Teen
Dropouts

Look for these and other books in the Lucent
Overview Series:

Teen Dropouts

by Elizabeth Weiss Vollstadt

TEEN ISSUES

To all caring teachers—and their students.

Acknowledgements

My thanks to career specialist Marilyn Smith and guidance counselor Steve Michaels of DeLand High School, DeLand, Florida, for answering my many questions and introducing me to new ideas and programs. Thanks also to the many other educators and program directors who shared their insights with me.

Library of Congress Cataloging-in-Publication Data

Vollstadt, Elizabeth Weiss, 1942–
    Teen dropouts / by Elizabeth Weiss Vollstadt.
        p.   cm. — (Lucent overview series. Teen issues)
    Includes bibliographical references and index.
    Summary: Discusses the problem of teen dropouts, including who drops out of school and why, what life is like after dropping out, how to help teens stay in school, and how to give them a second chance.
    ISBN 1-56006-625-3 (lib. bdg. : alk. paper)
    1. High school dropouts—United States—Juvenile literature. 2. High school attendance—United States—Juvenile literature. [1. Dropouts. 2. High school. 3. Schools.] I. Title. II. Series.
LC146.6.V64   2000
373.12'913'0973—dc21   99-042535

Copyright © 2000 by Lucent Books, Inc.
P.O. Box 289011, San Diego, CA 92198-9011
Printed in the U.S.A.

Contents

Introduction

What happens to a dream deferred?
Does it dry up
like a raisin in the sun? . . .
Or does it explode?[1]

THESE LINES ARE taken from the poem "Harlem" by African-American poet Langston Hughes. Written in 1951, the poem asks what happens when people cannot achieve their dreams because of racial prejudice. More recently, it inspired the title of a 1995 report on high school dropouts by the Educational Testing Service (ETS)—*Dreams Deferred: High School Dropouts in the United States*. The report uses some of the latest information from the National Center for Education Statistics (NCES) of the U.S. Department of Education to discuss the hundreds of thousands of young people who drop out of school each year.

The dreams of these young dropouts are said to be "deferred," or postponed, because more and more jobs today require a high level of skill and education. By dropping out of high school, teens are "locking themselves out of mainstream society and are barred from good-paying jobs,"[2] says the ETS. For example, according to the U.S. Bureau of the Census, in 1996 high school dropouts earned an average salary of only $14,013, about one-third less than the $21,431 earned by high school graduates. In addition, dropouts comprise half of all heads of households on welfare and more than half of all people in jail.

Despite these sobering facts, 5 percent of all teens in high school drop out each year. This percentage has remained fairly stable over the past ten years. While it may not seem high, in 1996 it represented 485,000 young people—almost half a million. Many of the 1996 dropouts were over eighteen, but almost half—43 percent—were only fifteen, sixteen, or seventeen years old.

It is also important to realize that if 5 percent of students drop out each year, the dropout rate for all four years of high school can be much higher. Four-year dropout rates are especially high in large urban districts. In 1992–1993, one out of four urban districts had a dropout rate that was greater than 35 percent. Dropout rates for Hispanic students exceed the national average and are among the highest in the nation. Dropout rates for African-American students also surpass the national average. Native Americans, too, have a high dropout rate, but because of their relatively small numbers government studies do not show them as a separate group.

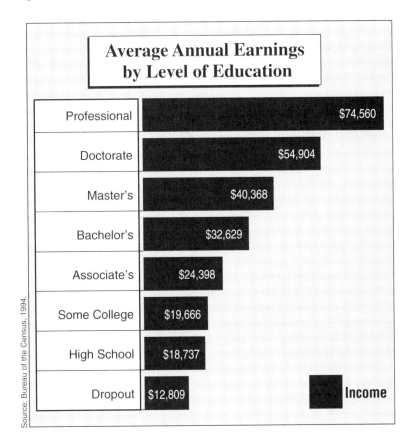

Source: Bureau of the Census, 1994.

Although students have varying reasons for dropping out of high school, many are overwhelmed by the pressure of performing well in school.

"I was invisible"

Why do students drop out of high school? Their reasons are many. Some are personal, such as pregnancy or the need to help support their families. Most, however, are school-related. Most students who dropped out were doing poorly in school, and many felt that their teachers didn't care. Only 18 percent reported to the NCES that they had passing grades in their last year of school. Often, dropouts felt that they didn't fit in, or they couldn't get along with their teachers or fellow students. One New York City teen told researcher Edwin Farrell:

> I think people drop out of school [because] of the pressure that school brings them. Like, sometimes the teacher might get on the back of a student so much that the student doesn't want to do the work. . . . And then that passes and he says, "I'm gonna start doing good. . . ." Then he's not doing as good as he's supposed to and when he sees his grade, he's, "you mean I'm doin' all that for nothin'? I'd rather not come to school."[3]

One student talked about older teens in school: "I think kids drop out of school because [they're getting] too old to be in high school. And . . . they think it's time to get a responsibility and to get a job and stuff."[4]

A teenager in Oakland, California, felt that no one in school cared about him:

> I was invisible, man. I knew it. I sat in those schools for two years. I sat in the back of the room and I did nothing. I didn't speak to anyone and no one spoke to me. Nobody said, "Do your work" or nothing. Then one day I said it, "Man I'm invisible here." I got up and walked out the door and I never went back.[5]

The young man in Oakland did find an alternative school where he was noticed and encouraged and was able to earn a high school diploma. But too many don't, and they end up with low-skill, low-paying jobs that offer no future. The costs are great, both to dropouts and to society. "Society cannot afford to lose the contributions these individuals have the potential to make," says Richard Coley, who wrote the ETS report. "Neither can society afford to pay for the dependencies that often follow dropping out of school. The nation can no longer afford to pay the price for 'dreams deferred.'"[6]

But teens will continue to drop out of school unless ways can be found to help them realize that education is the key to achieving a successful life. Working together, teens and educators can explore who drops out and why and then look for ways to help all young people stay in school and receive the education they need.

1

Who Drops Out
of School?

WHO ARE THE five hundred thousand teens who
drop out each year? For the most part, they are students
who are not succeeding in school. They often feel out of
place, that they don't belong. They may come from troubled families. They rarely participate in school sports or
activities. They may cut classes or not come to school at
all, but they do not necessarily misbehave in class. Only a
small percentage drop out because they are suspended or
expelled. One guidance counselor sees them as troubled
students who are easily overlooked:

> They're the kids that are just kind of like a ghost. They're
> never really recognized as being an outstanding student nor a
> non-achiever. They're the ones who are just kind of in the
> middle. And I think one of the main functions of the potential
> dropout is that they tend to remain anonymous at all times as
> much as possible.[7]

Another educator, the director of an independent living
center for teens, believes that potential dropouts are students who don't see school as making a difference in their
lives. They're not doing well, she says, and they don't see
any way to make things better:

> Mostly, they don't feel that they're making it in school any-
> more. And that there isn't anybody there that's on their side—
> that they can see. There might be some people there that care
> about them, but they may not know it. And if they don't feel
> it, it's not there for them. . . . And so they're not sensing that
> they're getting anything out of it. And they'd rather not be
> there. 'Cause they don't feel good in school.[8]

Some dropouts might be like Thomas,* whose parents separated when he was in the fourth grade. Even though he wanted his high school diploma, he started cutting classes when the work became difficult and he couldn't find anyone to help him. Eventually, he got a job and just dropped out. Or they might be like Kathy, who moved to a new school. It was hard being in a new class, not knowing her classmates or her teachers. When she started not doing well, she didn't know how to ask for help. She felt the teachers wouldn't stop to help just one person. She fell further behind and then started skipping school. Her mother was upset, but Kathy still wouldn't return to school.

Other dropouts might be succeeding in school, but family needs make it difficult to stay. Enrique is a good example. Enrique came to Texas from Mexico with his parents when he was ten years old. A bright boy, he learned English well enough to succeed in his classes. In eighth grade he was selected for the National Honor Society and was recommended for high-level classes in high school. But his parents, who had jobs as migrant farmworkers in Florida, needed financial help. As the only son without a job, Enrique was pressured by his older brothers to leave school and go to Florida to help his parents in the fields. A few years later he was back in Texas, working in a restaurant and still struggling to get his high school diploma.

If they are girls, teen dropouts might also be mothers. Almost one-third of all girls who drop out of school are pregnant or already have a child. One teen mother talks about trying to finish school: "I was 17. I got pregnant. I tried to complete school for three years. . . . I needed one class to graduate from high school. They wanted me to go eight hours a day. I refused. They kept on. I dropped out."[9]

Characteristics of dropouts

Each of these teens has his or her own story. But each one also shares characteristics with many other dropouts, such as economic status, personal problems, or the inability to deal

*Author's Note: The names of many of the students discussed in this book have been changed to preserve their privacy.

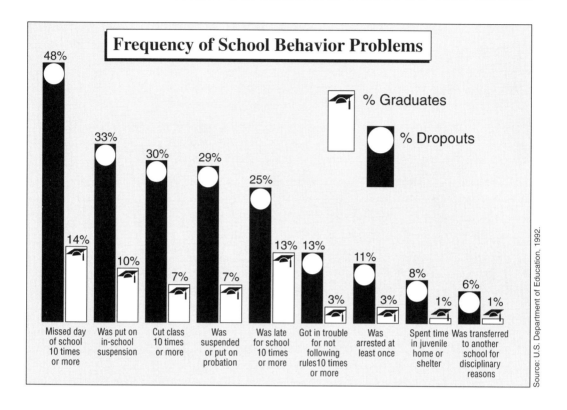

Frequency of School Behavior Problems

% Graduates

% Dropouts

- Missed day of school 10 times or more: 48% / 14%
- Was put on in-school suspension: 33% / 10%
- Cut class 10 times or more: 30% / 7%
- Was suspended or put on probation: 29% / 7%
- Was late for school 10 times or more: 25% / 13%
- Got in trouble for not following rules 10 times or more: 13% / 3%
- Was arrested at least once: 11% / 3%
- Spent time in juvenile home or shelter: 8% / 1%
- Was transferred to another school for disciplinary reasons: 6% / 1%

Source: U.S. Department of Education, 1992.

with the demands of school. Like Thomas and Enrique, dropouts are likely to come from low-income families and to be members of a minority group. (Asian-Americans are the exception, with a low dropout rate.) Teens in single-parent homes or in homes where English is not the primary language are also more at risk of dropping out. So are students whose parents dropped out themselves. Many of these parents do value education and want what is best for their children. But they are "so constrained by their own lack of education, mental and physical health, and financial resources that they [can] do little to help their adolescent children,"[10] say researchers Harriett D. Romo and Toni Falbo in their book, *Latino High School Graduation.*

Some dropouts come from troubled families where drugs and alcohol are abused. Some have suffered physical abuse. "[My mom] was a very abusive parent," says one dropout. "She used to beat me and stuff. It was hard . . . to get up and go to school."[11]

Another dropout talks about being constantly put down by his family. It is hard for teens to concentrate on schoolwork when faced with overwhelming personal problems. Still other dropouts have learning and behavioral problems that make schoolwork difficult. Or they disrupt classrooms with their behavior and set in motion a cycle of continuous problems with teachers and school, which sometimes leads to suspension or expulsion.

Some dropouts have no extraordinary problems, but, like Kathy, have problems adjusting to a new school. Sometimes, even talented, gifted students drop out. These "underachievers" often have learning styles that don't fit in with the way schools are organized. They are frustrated by the lack of opportunity to follow their own interests, ignore work that doesn't interest them, receive low grades, and eventually drop out.

Students with low academic skills

Most dropouts, however, have low academic skills. Like Thomas and Kathy, they are not doing well. Often they have so few credits that graduation seems impossible. In their study of Hispanic students in Austin, Texas, researchers Romo and Falbo studied the academic performance of "at-risk" students. Students at risk of dropping out, they said, have one or more of the following characteristics: they were left back at least one grade, scored two or more years below grade level in reading and math, failed at least two courses in one semester, or failed at least one section of a statewide test of basic skills.

The students they followed were fifteen years old when the study began. Almost one-fourth of them were still in middle school. "Many of the students in our sample had already begun the process of dropping out of school when we began our study," write Romo and Falbo. "Some of our students never made it to high school classrooms."[12]

Low-income teens

Many dropouts come from low-income families. The NCES states that in 1996 only 2.1 percent of students from high-income families dropped out of school, while five times as many students—11.1 percent—from low-income families dropped out. In addition, a large majority of early dropouts—those who leave school between grades eight and ten—are from poorer families. They often don't have the same preparation for success in school as middle-class children.

For example, one important part of being ready for school is being familiar with words and books. Yet many children in poor families do not have books in their homes. They are unlikely to attend preschool, and their parents don't read to them the way middle-class parents do. Some come to school unable to connect words and pictures. According to an article in *Youth & Society*, poor families are more dependent on schools to give their children a solid educational foundation. When this doesn't happen, or when children aren't successful in their early years at school, high school becomes even more frustrating.

Students are more likely to drop out of school if they are performing poorly academically or failing classes.

> Indeed, many poor and minority youngsters never experience success as learners from their entry into school, through their transition to the middle and high school. Such histories of academic frustration and failure among adolescents culminate [result] in low motivation, low expectation for future academic performance, and increasingly poor attendance, which finally results in dropout.[13]

Sometimes even students like Enrique, who are doing well, are forced to leave school to help support their families. As income and economic status increases, students are less likely to drop out. In fact, one government report says that when "blacks and whites from similar social backgrounds are compared . . . dropout rates for blacks are not higher, and in some cases may be lower, than those for whites."[14]

Being poor does not mean that a teen will drop out. In fact, almost 90 percent of low-income teens did stay in school in 1996. But the risk of dropping out is higher and such teens have more obstacles—lack of preparation, limited access to tools such as computers, a need to work to help their family—to overcome.

Minority teens

Minority teens are at higher risk of dropping out than white Americans. Hispanics have the highest rate of dropping out, followed by African-Americans, with white Americans having the lowest rate. The difference between whites and African-Americans is getting smaller, however, and dropout rates for both groups have gone down 40 percent over the past twenty-five years.

But this same decline is not seen among Hispanics. The U.S. Bureau of the Census reports that in 1996, 29.4 percent of Hispanics between the ages of sixteen and twenty-four who no longer attended school did not have high school diplomas. Contrast this with African-Americans, where only 13 percent didn't graduate, or with white Americans, where just 7.3 percent didn't have diplomas.

An additional problem for Hispanics is that they are likely to drop out after fewer years of school than either

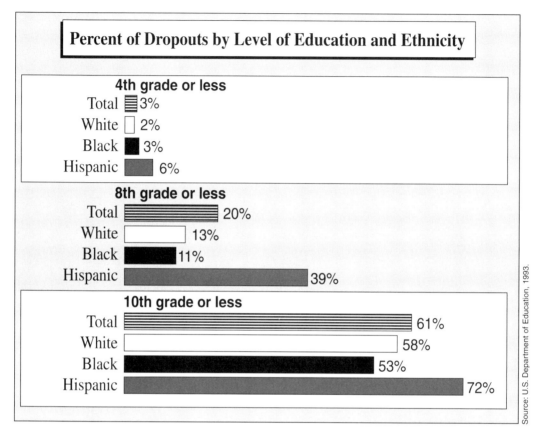

Percent of Dropouts by Level of Education and Ethnicity

4th grade or less

Total 3%
White 2%
Black 3%
Hispanic 6%

8th grade or less

Total 20%
White 13%
Black 11%
Hispanic 39%

10th grade or less

Total 61%
White 58%
Black 53%
Hispanic 72%

Source: U.S. Department of Education, 1993.

whites or African-Americans. Almost forty percent of Hispanic dropouts have less than an eighth-grade education, a much greater percentage than the thirteen percent of whites and eleven percent of African-Americans. Most discouraging, the dropout rate for Hispanic children whose parents were born in the United States is even higher than for children of immigrants. This means that the problem is not getting better over time.

Migrant farmworkers

One group of Hispanic teens, migrant farmworkers, has the greatest dropout rate of all—estimated at 45 percent. Migrant farmworkers are people who move from place to place to work on farms. Approximately 3 to 5 million migrants work on U.S. farms each year, and at least two-thirds of them are Hispanic.

In addition to the usual problems faced by minority students, migrant farmworkers move around constantly, another risk factor for dropping out. A U.S. Department of Education study that followed one class through high school found that dropouts had moved or changed schools more frequently than students who graduated. Changing schools means that students must adjust to new teachers, new classmates, and new material. They may be learning about the American Revolution in one school and find that their next school is already on the Civil War.

University of South Florida researchers Yolanda Martinez and Ann Cranston-Gingras discuss the problems of migrant teens in a 1996 article for *High School Journal*. They found that the more times a student moved, the more likely he or she was to drop out of school. In addition, students who disliked moving were more likely to drop out than those who saw moving as a challenge or a way to have more experiences.

The children of farmworkers have the highest dropout rates of any student group because they must constantly move to where their parents can find work. Here field workers harvest lettuce in Salinas, California.

Even when enrolled in school, migrant worker teens are often absent. Sometimes they help their parents pick crops; other times they take care of younger brothers and sisters. The absences are rarely a choice—they are necessary for the family to survive. Martinez and Cranston-Gingras discuss the low income of migrant workers and the need for children to help:

> In order for the family to survive economically, migrant children and young adults must contribute to the family income. This economic contribution means not only travelling with their parents to where work is available, but also working long hours before and after school and on weekends and holidays. During high peak seasons when work is abundant, many children miss school completely to care for younger siblings or to work in the fields themselves.[15]

Finding themselves far behind, or constantly feeling like an outsider in a new school, migrant students too often find it easier to drop out than to persist.

Urban African-Americans

Hispanics are not the only group whose dropout rate remains high. Poor, disadvantaged African-Americans who live in the inner city also drop out in large numbers. In 1993, for example, many urban school districts had a four-year dropout rate of 35 percent. In addition, more than 70 percent of the urban districts in the same study reported an increase in their annual dropout rates among both African-American and Hispanic students. Educator William Boyd writes in the *Teachers College Record* that "disadvantaged youth concentrated in our inner cities represent the most imperiled portion of our growing population of at-risk students."[16]

It is no surprise that these young people are so imperiled. They often come from single-parent families. Unemployment is high in their neighborhoods, where middle-class and even working-class families have moved away. Some children reach their teens without seeing any families with a steady breadwinner. As a result, they don't see the relationship between school and future employment.

Teenagers in the inner city also face problems of safety. Violent crime is a fact of life, often associated with illegal drugs and teenage gangs. Sometimes, just getting to and from school safely is a challenge. Teens have even been killed for the clothes they were wearing. In such a dangerous environment, it is difficult to concentrate on schoolwork. One minister in Chicago is quoted as saying, "Playtime doesn't exist down here. Trying to lead a child's life is fraught [filled] with danger. There is a lot of isolationism and secrecy and fear."[17]

Teenagers who live in inner cities are more likely to drop out of school.

Some teens don't even believe they have a future. One student in Chicago reports that six of his friends have been killed since grade school. The idea of delayed gratification—working hard now in order to achieve a better future—seems pointless. For such teens, dropping out of school can seem to be a logical decision.

Students facing cultural pressures

Most students drop out of school because they are doing poorly. But sometimes, even successful students feel pressure to abandon the hard work and concentration on academic skills that school requires. This is especially prevalent among African-American youth from troubled urban communities, where the relationship between success in school and success in American society has not always been clear. Too many of these young people equate following school rules and doing well academically with being white or "acting white," says William Boyd. Because of this attitude, he adds, working hard and succeeding in school are not considered to be "socially acceptable—at least not without some social and personal costs."[18]

The story of Marvin Wilson is a good example. A talented student, Marvin was part of a class at Belmont Elementary School in Philadelphia that attracted national attention in the 1980s. At that time, a couple named George and Diane Weiss promised to send to college all members of Marvin's elementary class who finished high school. In 1989, as a high school student, Marvin was an honored guest of President George Bush and presented the president with a "Say Yes to Education" T-shirt. Yet three months later, he nearly dropped out of school. Even after special attention and counseling, Marvin still found it difficult to go to school.

Other pressures

According to Diane Weiss, he was getting two different messages. One was from the school: to stay in school and look ahead to a future that included graduation and college; the other was on the streets and from his friends: to live for today and not worry about school or the future. "They're so conflicting, so difficult," Weiss says, "no wonder he's so horribly confused."[19]

Marvin himself felt that his accomplishments might work against him. "If I told my friends [that I had met the president], they wouldn't believe me," he says. "I don't want to tell people what I do good, just what I do normal."[20] Marvin's story is important because it shows that many high school dropouts don't lack intelligence or the ability to do the necessary work for a high school diploma.

Teen dropouts come from a variety of ethnic and economic backgrounds.

Other pressures—from school, from families, from friends—cause them to drop out.

Faces of dropouts

There is no single answer to the question of who drops out of school. The faces of teen dropouts mirror the faces of America—white Americans, African-Americans, Hispanics, Asian-Americans, Native Americans. Most minority groups have a larger percentage of students dropping out than whites, but, because they are a majority, white Americans still drop out in greater numbers. In 1996, for example, 267,000 white students dropped out of school, more than the number of African-Americans and Hispanics combined.

It is also true that even among high-risk groups—such as migrant farmworkers and poor urban African-Americans— more than half do manage to graduate. Researchers are looking at schools, families, and students themselves to find out what makes the difference between success and failure—why some students graduate while others drop out.

2

Why Teens Drop Out

I wasn't interested; I didn't care. You know, I just wanted to go and have fun. I wanted to see my friends and I wanted to go party. And I wanted to have a social life. But I could not make school into a social life . . . so I would "ditch" [cut school] all the time.[21]

Sometimes I didn't know how to do the school work or I didn't feel like it. My friends encouraged me to go with them to the movies. I made all Fs (failing grades) and that was discouraging. I like fun and attention.[22]

School was boring because they were not teaching me what I needed to know. They were not teaching what will help me in the real world.[23]

There were too many diversions in school. There were groups of kids that socialize all the time. If you didn't fit in, they looked down on you.[24]

I had to help out my family for a while 'cause money matters were getting a little tight.[25]

I dropped out of school when I was eighteen in the eleventh grade and I was pregnant. And I got married.[26]

TEENS GIVE MANY reasons for dropping out of school. They're bored, they're failing, they want to party, they can't see how their courses will help them in life, they have problems with other students, they have serious family troubles, they need a job, they're pregnant. Most dropouts didn't like school and were doing poorly. Over 80 percent had failed their last year in school.

The most comprehensive study to date of why students drop out is a U.S. Department of Education study that followed a group of students from eighth grade in 1988 through high school graduation in 1992. It showed that the top two reasons for dropping out involved school problems: "didn't like school" (44%) and "was getting poor grades" (39%). Other school-related reasons were "couldn't keep up with schoolwork" (30%) and "couldn't get along with teachers" (26%). Personal problems were also significant, but they were not named by as many students. The problems included "got a job" (27%), "felt I didn't belong (24%), and "became a parent" (17%).[27]

While boys and girls dropped out at about the same rate, the study found that their reasons were different. Richard Coley discusses the study in *Dreams Deferred:* "Males were more likely to drop out because of school problems,

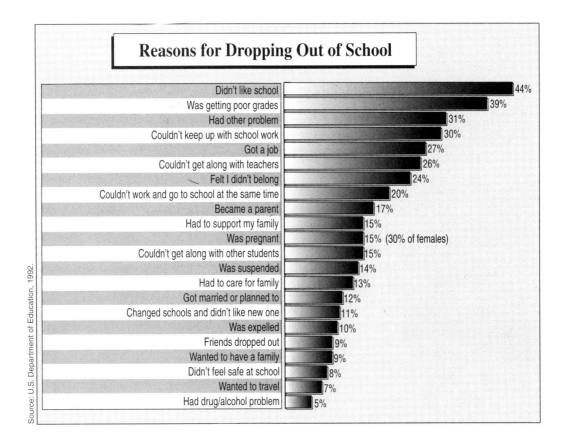

Reasons for Dropping Out of School

Didn't like school	44%
Was getting poor grades	39%
Had other problem	31%
Couldn't keep up with school work	30%
Got a job	27%
Couldn't get along with teachers	26%
Felt I didn't belong	24%
Couldn't work and go to school at the same time	20%
Became a parent	17%
Had to support my family	15%
Was pregnant	15% (30% of females)
Couldn't get along with other students	15%
Was suspended	14%
Had to care for family	13%
Got married or planned to	12%
Changed schools and didn't like new one	11%
Was expelled	10%
Friends dropped out	9%
Wanted to have a family	9%
Didn't feel safe at school	8%
Wanted to travel	7%
Had drug/alcohol problem	5%

Source: U.S. Department of Education, 1992.

including being suspended and expelled, and for reasons having to do with work. Females were more likely to quit school to have a baby or get married. It is particularly striking that nearly one-third of the females quit school because they got pregnant."[28]

A smaller study in Austin, Texas, by educators Harriett Romo and Toni Falbo asked the question, "If you know students who are seriously considering dropping out of school or who have already dropped out, why do you think they are dropping out?" The top four responses were "lack of interest in school" (53%), "serious personal problems" (39%), "serious family problems" (34%), and "poor grades" (29%).[29]

School problems, then, are at the top of almost all lists of reasons that teens drop out of school. School problems have many causes: Sometimes students make poor choices, sometimes schools don't meet all the needs of their students, and sometimes students have problems in their personal lives that make school attendance difficult or even impossible.

Poor choices

Dropping out is rarely a snap decision made for one reason alone. Most experts agree that it is a process that often begins with students dropping out mentally. They stop paying attention in class, stop doing their homework, cut classes, and finally, don't go to school at all. When they actually drop out, they are just making official something that has already happened.

What starts this process? Sometimes it begins with the student making poor choices. The girl who "ditches" school to party and socialize, for example, is making a poor choice. So is the boy who goes to the movies with his friends instead of doing his schoolwork. Another poor choice is made by the boy who says, "I just went [to the recreation center] and played basketball one day and just got into a habit. Forget school—I'll just play basketball. And I just kept doing that every day—and then I got kicked out."[30]

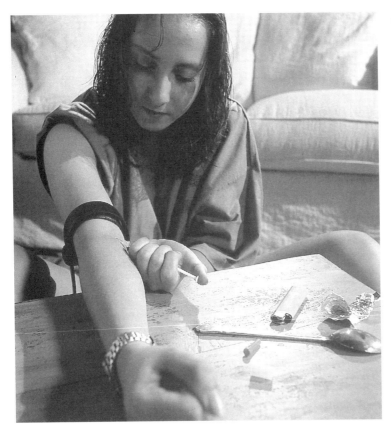

A teenage girl shoots up to get high. Teens who become heavily involved in drugs often choose to drop out of school.

Drug use is yet another poor choice some teens make. Drug use takes over a person's life and makes other obligations, including school, unimportant. Users cut classes to spend their time looking for and using drugs. Sometimes they are suspended; other times they fail their courses because they are not there to do the work. Because it is illegal, drug use also makes the teen a criminal in the eyes of the law. Some students drop out when they get into trouble with the police.

These teens have not accepted the responsibility they have to become productive adults. It is very likely they will start getting bad grades. Then they will become less interested in school and cut classes more often. Eventually they will fail and have to repeat their courses. Graduation will remain a distant goal. As time goes by, it will be easier to give up and drop out.

Large, impersonal schools

Many educators believe that teens wouldn't make such poor choices if schools offered more personal attention. Too often, teens with problems don't get the help they need. In a large school with large classes, teachers have limited time to spend with each student. Troublemakers get attention, as do high achievers. But those in the middle, who are struggling quietly, can go unnoticed. Sometimes busy schools don't even inform parents of frequent absences.

"I think we create the dropout problem," says Kitty Kelly Epstein, professor of education at Holy Names College in Oakland, California, and former teacher at an alternative school. "Many of today's high schools are large and impersonal. Teachers often have six classes and one hundred and fifty students. The students are anonymous. There's no adult responsible for them. No one follows what they're doing."[31]

Most students do succeed in large, modern high schools. They have parents with the skills to monitor their schoolwork and find help when needed. But not all families can offer this support; some teenagers have no one but school to help them. Some students state that they stayed in school because of help from friends or a specific teacher, coach, guidance counselor, or even principal. But when they can't find this support, students are left to try alone.

In a 1992 study of twenty high school dropouts in Oakland, Epstein found that most talked about "the anonymity, the uncaring, and the humiliation experienced in school."[32] Thomas, one young man in her study, came from a family with serious problems. His father had lost his job and his parents had divorced. In high school, Thomas found his coursework to be difficult but he couldn't find the help he needed. When he wanted to see his guidance counselor, he had to wait in line. Then, he says, "When I did see him he was always ready to go to lunch. That just showed me right there that he didn't care. Finally, when he did talk to me he told me I wasn't going to graduate."[33] Thomas started hanging around with the wrong people and cutting classes. Eventually, he dropped out completely. He later graduated from a smaller, alternative school.

School is boring

Thomas started cutting classes because he was doing poorly. Many other teens say that they skip school or drop out because school is boring. They may not find their classes relevant to their lives, or they may not be interested in a particular subject. They may not like their teachers or the way their teachers conduct their classes. One teen who dropped out of school says, "Everything was basically straightforward. Sit down, read the book, answer questions. Nothing that would really catch your attention or keep you from falling asleep."[34] Another teen says, "I was absent a lot of times. . . . I was just bored with the whole thing. It seemed like nobody was payin' attention to me."[35]

At some point, all students—even those with straight A's—say that school is boring. Yet most students do not

Some teen dropouts cite boredom as their reason for leaving school.

drop out. In his book *Hanging In and Dropping Out*, teacher and researcher Edwin Farrell suggests that, to students doing poorly, being bored is a way to feel good about themselves. They are bored with school because they find no role for themselves. They have found no teacher to believe in them, they have failed repeatedly, and perhaps they have been held back from moving on to the next grade. They feel pressure to succeed, but don't believe they can. When they say that school is no good—that school is boring—it removes the pressure and the responsibility to try.

Farrell talks about a girl who dropped out: "If a student, from past experience, believes that her output will be less than successful, she might well prefer to invest her energy outside of school and deal with school by being

A girl yawns during class. Some students find school boring because they don't believe they can succeed.

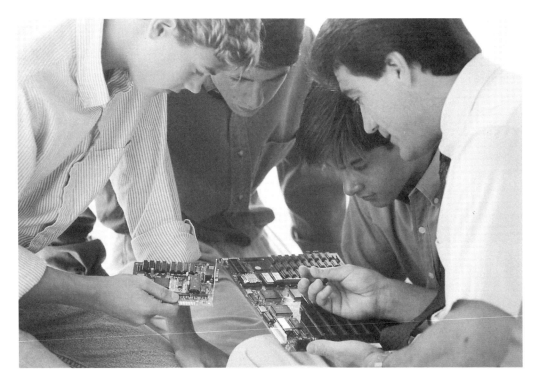

bored."[36] Successful students, on the other hand, can put up with boring classes because they are receiving some reward in the form of good grades. They also have good relationships with their teachers and feel as if they are part of the school.

Lack of "real life" courses

Another reason students say they are bored is that they can't see a relationship between their classes and their future. In American high schools today, much emphasis is placed on preparation for college. Teens on a college-prep track do not have to make career decisions yet. They have a "four-year moratorium [period of delay] . . . to develop their career selves," writes Farrell. But not all students have this luxury, especially if they are poor or from families where college is not expected. These teens, he says, "are more concerned with job skills than Shakespeare, employment possibilities than French verbs, meaningful work than debating."[37]

Teenage boys take apart a computer in a vocational computer training program. Many students who are not college bound are more interested in learning job skills than academic subjects.

Some of these students might even need a job to help support their families, but they don't see how their high school diploma will help them get a better job. For example, almost half of the teens in Romo and Falbo's study said that their friends in a school/work program remained in the same minimum-wage, part-time jobs even after they graduated. Some inner-city teens don't see jobs for themselves at all, with or without a diploma.

Peer pressure

Such widespread attitudes about school lead to a teen culture that does not value high school or the diploma it awards. This peer culture is strong. Studies have shown that teens are more likely to drop out when they have friends or siblings who do. Even students who are doing well can feel pressure from their peers to conform. They start to hide their achievements or stop doing their schoolwork entirely. Eventually they drop out.

A negative peer culture is especially strong among minorities. They often feel they do not fit in with the white middle-class values of the school. Even today, many inner-city African-Americans cannot find jobs. They don't see a connection between school and success. As a result, doing well in school is considered "acting white" and is not respected.

Hispanics, too, often belong to peer groups in which schoolwork is not valued. Many believe that schools don't encourage them to succeed. "Some [Hispanic] students don't feel teachers care about them or understand their culture,"[38] says Alma Maya, who works for a Bridgeport, Connecticut, chapter of Aspira, a national advocacy group for Hispanic youth. They see that the high achievers are middle-class white students and they associate working hard in school with being "nerdy" or "Anglo." One Hispanic girl living in Santa Fe, New Mexico, says that when she cut school, she was only doing what was expected, "In school, they make you feel like a dumb Mexican."[39] Students react by banding together and rejecting the values of the school.

Another source of peer pressure is the gang. Some teens having trouble at home or with schoolwork turn to gangs to find "family," to be popular, and to feel good about who they are. Unfortunately, gangs encourage behaviors such as cutting classes, not doing homework, or skipping school completely. Gang members also get involved in fights in school, which leads to suspension or expulsion. Some gangs require stealing or other crimes before someone can be a full-fledged member. Not all gang members drop out of school, but being in a gang increases a teen's chance of neglecting schoolwork and dropping out.

Family problems

Strong families can help students resist peer pressure. These families can also support and encourage their teenagers to work hard for a better future. But many teens today do not have strong families. In fact, personal and family problems are a major factor in students doing poorly in school and dropping out. Many teens today face problems at home such as poverty, divorce, illness, alcoholism, drug abuse, and sometimes even physical or sexual abuse. Some may blame themselves for their parents' divorce or for other problems. Some may not have enough to eat; others come to school without having slept all night. When faced with such overwhelming problems, students find it difficult, if not impossible, to concentrate on schoolwork. The failure that results eventually leads to dropping out.

In her book *Full-Service Schools*, Joy Dryfoos says,

> We know a great deal about "high-risk" children. Their status is defined by their families; they lack attention from parents who can provide nurturing and attention. . . . Parental substance abuse adversely affects offspring. . . . addicted parents are also poor role models and may be negligent and even abusive. We know, too, that poverty erodes expectations and that families have difficulty raising children in stressful, dangerous, and unhealthy environments. And, of course, children of absent parents suffer most of all, unless they are attached to a strong adult who can act as a surrogate [substitute] parent.[40]

Educator Cyndi Terry sees the "decline of the family unit" as a key factor in many problems children and teens face, both in school and in their personal lives. "Kids no longer have the support of the family unit," she says. "In many cases, even their basic needs, such as the need for shelter, aren't being met. Some kids don't know whether they're going to stay at grandma's house, a center, or even if Mom is going to be evicted." With such uncertainty in their daily lives, learning reading and math can become

Family problems often leave teenagers preoccupied and unable to focus at school.

secondary. They fall further and further behind. "Then," she continues, "with overcrowded classes, the struggling child doesn't get the attention he or she needs."[41] For these teens, dropping out of school may seem like the only option.

Like most educators, Terry is careful not to blame parents for these problems. She believes that most parents love their children and want what's best for them. But the parents are often so overwhelmed by their own problems that they can't give their children or teenagers the structure, support, and attention they need.

Need to work or help the family

In fact, it sometimes becomes the responsibility of teenagers to help their families. Almost one-third of teens give work as a reason for dropping out. Sometimes this means a part-time job, which cuts down on study time. Sometimes the teen drops out of school to take a full-time job. Boys especially feel pressure to help support their families, with 35 percent reporting that they left school to take a job.

Helping to financially support the family is especially common among low-income Hispanics. When Enrique's parents weren't earning enough to support themselves, the family pressure he faced to leave school, where he was doing well, and help them was not unusual. Enrique's older brother explains that many young people in their community leave school to help at home. He says, "They dedicate themselves to work and leave studying, rightly so, because they have to help their parents work."[42]

Girls face different family expectations. Often, girls in poor, minority families are expected to take care of younger brothers and sisters or parents who are sick. Or, if they become pregnant themselves, they drop out to take care of their own babies.

Pregnancy

Almost one-third of girls give pregnancy as their reason for dropping out of school. Researcher Kathleen Kaminski

Many girls who become pregnant drop out of school.

found the percentage in her study of rural dropouts to be 60 percent. These are high figures, especially since federal law makes it illegal for schools to suspend pregnant girls or to discriminate against them in any way. Why, then, do so many pregnant girls drop out of school?

One reason is lack of child care. Unless a girl has a supportive family—often a mother or older sister who does not work—it is hard to find someone to care for the baby. Kaminski writes that almost all of the girls she talked to would have stayed in school if they could have found day care for their babies. In some families, too, girls are expected to leave school when they are pregnant. In others, the family is so angry that they refuse to help their daughter. Finishing school is difficult for many teens under the best circumstances. Having a baby to take of can make it impossible.

Some girls drop out of school to get married when they are pregnant. They think that they will not have to worry about finding a job anymore. Researchers have found, too, that some pregnant girls drop out because they do not want to stay in school anyway. They are doing poorly, they do not think a high school diploma is important, or they do not think they will ever succeed in getting one, and pregnancy can be a good excuse to leave.

Being held back

Students leave school, too, when they have been held back a grade, or maybe even two. They are older than most of their classmates and graduation seems far away. Many dropouts were held back when they were in school—some were held back twice. Their reasons for failure are varied: Some may have started school without any reading preparation. Some may have learning disabilities. Others may have problems at home that keep them from concentrating.

Most experts agree that being held back one year increases a student's risk of dropping out. Being held back two years makes dropping out almost a certainty. Studies also show that students believe they are harmed by being held back. One study states, "Schoolchildren rank grade retention [being held back] as one of the worst things that can happen to a child, just below death of a parent and going blind."[43]

Researcher Edwin Farrell writes, "A 17-year-old who has only enough credits to be a ninth grader may see little chance of graduating. With little hope, anyone with common sense might avoid failure by refusing to participate in the system."[44] Many older teens do just that. In 1996, students age nineteen or older had the highest dropout rate.

Educators realize that students cannot be passed along from grade to grade if they don't have the required skills. In most cases, social promotion—that is, advancing a student who cannot read, write, or do basic math at grade level—leaves a student no better prepared than if that student had dropped out of school. But many educators believe that new ways, other than grade retention, must be found to ensure that students learn. Romo and Falbo suggest that the answer might lie in new teaching methods or more hours spent in school, especially hours spent on math and reading. In addition, they say, rather than have a student repeat an entire year, tutoring that focuses on a student's specific problem areas should be offered after school, on Saturdays, and during the summer.

Washington Post columnist David Broder reports on an elementary school in St. Petersburg, Florida, in which such special help has been successful. When thirty-two children in a kindergarten class failed to meet word recognition standards for promotion, traditional policy would have meant they repeated kindergarten. Instead, they were promoted into smaller classes and given extra help and tutor-

ing. By May of their first-grade year, all were reading at grade level. More research needs to be done, especially with high school students, but it is clear already that grade retention does not solve problems for failing students. It only makes them more likely to drop out.

Special problems of minorities

Many problems that contribute to dropping out, such as pregnancy or poor performance, exist across racial and cultural lines. But minorities face additional problems. Schools can contribute to their lack of success by expecting less from them, especially if the students are poor. Poor children rarely have the school readiness of middle-class children, and they score lower on standardized tests. This puts them in lower learning tracks where the work is easier and less challenging. Both Hispanics and African-Americans are more likely to be in low tracks than white students. When teachers expect less of students, the students expect less of themselves. Researchers Romo and Falbo state that being tracked into low-level courses promotes "apathy [not caring], feelings of exclusion, and disregard about completing classroom tasks and doing assigned work."[45]

Lack of proficiency in English leads some teens to drop out of school.

Language problems also make school more difficult, and language problems tend to be more common among low-income Hispanics. Lupe is a good example. She came to the United States from Mexico with her parents when she was ten years old. Her parents spoke only Spanish, and she lived in a neighborhood where English was heard only on television. Even though Lupe attended an American school and was in a bilingual program, she didn't feel comfortable using English. She couldn't keep up in high school and failed her courses. It was easy to just stop going. When she officially dropped out, she had no credits toward graduation.

Many states today are raising graduation standards and requiring students to pass statewide tests in order to graduate. Some Hispanic teens give up on school and drop out when they realize they do not have the language skills to pass those tests and receive their diplomas.

Value of a high school diploma

For many teenagers finding reasons to drop out of school is easier than finding reasons to stay—until they look at the future. The chances of finding a good job and achieving financial success are slim without a high school diploma. High school graduates earn one-third more than dropouts and the gap is widening. Between 1975 and 1992, the earnings of graduates rose 150 percent, while the earnings of dropouts only doubled. Graduates have a lower unemployment rate and are more likely to receive training and promotions. A high school diploma also opens the door to further education, which is a key to success in today's economy.

Teens who drop out of school have not solved their problems. They have entered a world with even more problems—a world of limited opportunity.

3

Life After Dropping Out

LIFE AFTER DROPPING OUT is difficult. With their lack of education and skills, dropouts are unable to find good, well-paying jobs. They are often concentrated in low-level positions, such as laborers or service workers. Even more discouraging, dropouts are almost twice as likely as graduates to have no job at all. One girl who dropped out of school says,

> At first I thought, OK, I'll go get a full-time job. But . . . I didn't have any skills that I needed to do those jobs. And the bad thing was, these jobs were simple. I mean, a secretary's job . . . you think, all I have to do is go in there and type. But if you don't know how to type, you find yourself paying for a course which, if you went back to school, it's free.[46]

The key word in her statement is *skills*: Good jobs today require skills. Thirty or forty years ago, when the parents or grandparents of today's teenagers were young, the dropout rate was higher than it is today. But at that time, even people without skills were able to find jobs that paid decent salaries and offered benefits such as health insurance and pensions. This is not necessarily true today.

Changing economy

The U.S. economy has changed from being a manufacturing economy to a service and information economy. A manufacturing economy has many industries producing goods such as cars, television sets, clothing, and countless

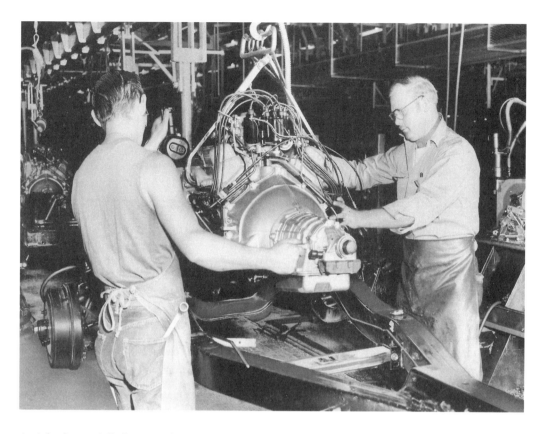

As jobs for unskilled workers diminish, higher education is more important to a successful future. Dropouts face an especially hard future, doomed to a life of low-paying, dead-end jobs.

other things that people use every day. In the past, many of those jobs were on assembly lines and didn't require a lot of education. Strong unions bargained for good salaries and benefits. Even a high school dropout could support his or her family.

Today, however, many of these low and semi-skilled manufacturing jobs have moved overseas, where wages are much lower. This change has affected the entire country, but has hit cities the hardest. For example, says Edwin Farrell in *Hanging In and Dropping Out*, "From 1970 to 1984, New York City lost 492,000 jobs that required less than a high school education and gained 239,000 jobs in which the average employee had some higher education."[47] Good jobs today require education—the traditional skills of reading, writing, and math, plus a working knowledge of computers. Manufacturing workers, too, must be better educated. They need to know how to learn and how to study.

Fast-changing technology means that workers must continue to learn new skills.

The automobile industry provides a good example of the increased skills needed in the labor force. An article in the *Economist* magazine says that the three biggest American car manufacturers (General Motors, Chrysler, and Ford) are becoming more particular about whom they hire. In 1994 only 80 percent of Ford's hourly workers had a high school diploma. But almost all of their newly hired employees had high school diplomas and a third had some college as well. Workers today need an education to do their jobs. According to the *Economist:*

> Work on the assembly line is becoming more intellectually demanding. Employees are now expected to spot and correct defects, even to suggest ways to improve quality and productivity. That means mastering some fairly sophisticated concepts, with fancy names such as Statistical Process Control and Continuous Improvement.[48]

Students attend a class to learn to operate a forklift. Today, as technology makes equipment more sophisticated, training is required even for unskilled jobs.

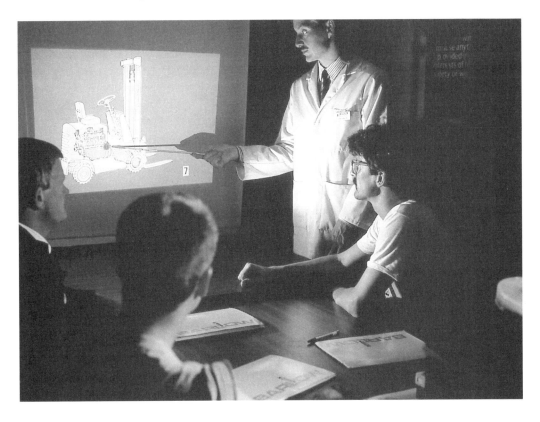

Financial reality

People without skills are left with low-paying service jobs. Chances for advancement are small or don't exist at all. In writing about his at-risk students, Farrell says, "The reality of the job market, then, for the at-risk student is (1) there are few jobs available for them, (2) those that are available are minimum-wage service jobs, (3) they have few skills and little knowledge to sell on the market, and (4) they have little access to whatever job network there is." [49]

The number of young Americans in that position is high. In October 1996 approximately 3.6 million young adults between the ages of sixteen and twenty-four who no longer attended school were without a high school diploma. They make up 11.1 percent of all people in that age group. Over their lifetimes, according to 1994 figures from the Bureau of the Census, these dropouts will earn $212,000 less than high school graduates, $384,000 less than people having some college, $812,000 less than college graduates, and $2,404,000 less than people with professional degrees.

Jobs for dropouts

For dropouts, just finding a job can be difficult. Many don't find jobs at all. The unemployment rate for dropouts is higher than that of graduates: 22.5 percent in 1995 versus 12.1 percent for high school graduates, according to the Bureau of Labor Statistics. Those who do find jobs work for low wages and have little chance for advancement. One teen says, "I was there in the big city, broke. Couldn't get a job without a GED certificate, a high school diploma. I looked. The only job I could find was passing out flyers all day in the hot sun." [50] Another teen had this experience:

> I did everything I could—for Kentucky Fried Chicken. . . . I worked for McDonald's for about three weeks. Then I had a variety of jobs. I worked in the fields. In the onion sheds myself, stacking fifty-pound bags of onions. My last job was with the city . . . for the park department. . . . I seen people there 15 years that were making maybe fifty cents more than I was, and it seemed [the job] was getting nowhere. [51]

Still another dropout, Matt, has a job making sandwiches at a coffee shop. He enjoys his job but is looking ahead for a future with more opportunities. He gives half of his paycheck to his father as a way of saving to attend a technical school.

The low pay, or for those who can't find a job at all, the lack of pay, makes it difficult to find a place to live. Rents are high, especially in big cities, and are often more than dropouts can afford. The lucky ones, like Matt, are able to live with their parents. But others are not so lucky. They may have alienated their families with disruptive behavior or drug use. Or they may have run away from problems at home. All too often, the freedom they seek is not what they envisioned. They end up on the street with nowhere to go. One boy says, "Just went day by day, anywhere I could stay. If I didn't stay anywhere, I lived on the street."[52]

In desperation, some teens turn to crime or prostitution. In fact, according to the Office of Juvenile Justice and Delinquency Prevention, dropouts account for three-quarters of the teens involved with the juvenile court system. "I found things to do," says one girl. "Mostly criminal things, like drugs." Another girl echoes, "I was a prostitute for a while. I did some porno stuff. I pulled a couple tricks off and on. I sold some dope." One boy got arrested. "Got busted. Breaking and entering. . . . It's not cool to be in trouble with the law. It's dumb."[53] Sometimes getting arrested can actually help a teen because he or she can receive professional help. Other times it can be the first of many arrests. Studies show that more than half of all people in prison are high school dropouts.

Welfare

Teen mothers who drop out of school find it even harder to earn a living. They cannot look for work if they don't have someone to care for their babies. Many end up on welfare. One welfare caseworker says that at least 50 percent of the people she sees coming through the system are high school dropouts. Marcia is just one example of a teen mother on welfare. She receives a monthly check, plus

Many teen mothers rely on welfare to support themselves and their children, but new limits on welfare will force many into the job market, often into low-paying jobs.

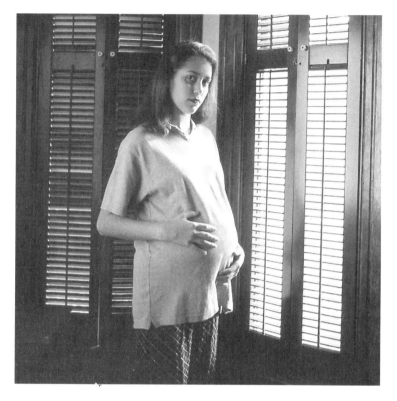

food stamps, to pay for food, rent, clothing, and any extras for herself and her baby. But it's not a lot. "There's no money left over to amount to anything,"[54] she says.

Marcia lives in a small, dreary apartment with her year-old son. One room serves as a living room, bedroom, and baby's room. A double bed dominates the room. It has no bedspread, just a dark sheet and two pillows with mismatched pillowcases. A table is just big enough to hold diapers and a small boom box. Marcia has no radio, no television. There are no curtains on the window, just a shade. A single chair is covered with a plain red blanket. Next to the chair is the baby's crib. Here, Marcia has attached a Winnie-the-Pooh mobile.

Marcia's kitchen is small and plain. An old-fashioned refrigerator with one door dominates the room. When she opens the door, she shows a small, ice-crusted freezer. The refrigerator vibrates, she says, and "sounds bad." The bathroom, too, has old-fashioned fixtures and a plain white tub and sink. There are no cabinets, just a small wooden table covered with soaps, shampoo, and other toiletries. A piece of blue material covers the single window. The only other item is a small space heater. "There's holes over there behind the tub from lots of water being dumped on it over the years," she says.[55]

Making life even more difficult for Marcia is the fact that changes in welfare laws now place a limit on the number of years she may receive payments. She will have to find a way to take advantage of any training that is available. Without an education, she will be locked into poverty.

Risks to dropouts

In addition to low-paying jobs, welfare, and dingy apartments, dropouts are more likely than graduates to engage in unhealthy behavior. A study of seven thousand teenagers by the U.S. Centers for Disease Control and Prevention (CDC) reports on smoking, drug use, and unprotected sex. The study found that dropouts are twice as likely to smoke marijuana and three times more likely to use cocaine. Seventy percent of dropouts reported having sex, versus 45 percent of teens still in school. This behavior often results in delinquency, crime, early pregnancy, and drug and alcohol abuse. Yet with all these threats to their health, dropouts are less likely than those in school to have access to health care and other social services.

Dropouts are also less likely to feel good about themselves. One dropout interviewed for the PBS documentary series *The Merrow Report* was asked, "When you look in the mirror at yourself, what do you see?" He replied, "When I look in the mirror, I see a guy right there that doesn't know his future, doesn't know what he's going to have in the future. That's all I see." When asked about his fears he replied, "Every day makes me feel afraid because I don't know what's coming to me in the future. My future, that's what I'm afraid of. . . . I might not have a home, kids, you know. I might be out in the street or something."[56] Another teen, who had returned to school, said about her time as a dropout, "I felt like a loser."[57] Feelings of low self-esteem can lead to a cycle of even more destructive behavior, such as drug and alcohol abuse.

The 1992 Department of Education study of one class found that dropouts differ from graduates in the amount of control they feel they have over their lives. This might be due to feelings of low self-esteem. It also might be because their low level of education and skills limits the choices they have when they look for jobs—and then their low salaries limit their choices in where and how they live. Along these same lines, almost half of all dropouts versus

Teen dropouts often have low self-esteem which adds to their lack of success in life.

one-quarter of graduates also agreed with the statement, "When I try to get ahead, something stops me." Dropouts are also more likely to believe that "Plans hardly ever work out."[58]

Chances of success as a dropout

While many at-risk teens have a fatalistic view of their chances for success, others have an overly optimistic view of what they can achieve without proper preparation. Some teens look at movie actors and athletes who didn't complete school and think that they, too, can succeed without a diploma. They see themselves being successful as football or basketball stars, making a lot of money. Working hard in school is for other people. But these ambitions are not realistic. The chances of becoming a sports hero are much too slim to consider seriously. The National Dropout Prevention Center offers these statistics about basketball players:

> Only one out of 68 high school basketball players [1.5%] will get to play on a Division 1 college varsity basketball team. Only one out of 12 Division 1 college basketball players [8.3%] will make it to the pros. A high school basketball player has about one chance in 840 [0.12%] to become a professional basketball player.[59]

Similar statistics are probably true for other sports and for the entertainment industry. They are not very good odds on which to build a future.

Looking ahead

In spite of all of the problems that dropouts have, the Department of Education study found that many recent dropouts are still optimistic about the future. About half felt that they would have a better life than their parents, and three-quarters believed their children would have a better life than they will have. They expect to have successful families and friendships.

However, Richard Coley suggests in *Dreams Deferred* that their optimism may be wishful thinking. "The statistics on their predecessors," he writes, "give little basis for

Some teens believe they can find success in professional sports and therefore don't need an education, but the odds of becoming a high-paying athlete are low.

optimism for large numbers of them. Dropouts have become damaged at a critical point in their lives; separated from an environment that was probably their best hope for a productive and rewarding life."[60]

Perhaps one reason for the optimism of these recent dropouts is that most of them expect to continue their education. Eighty-five percent of teens in the same study expected to get a high school diploma eventually. Each year, about half a million people receive GED (General Education Development) high school equivalency certificates. Others return to their high schools. Still others find alternative programs. Those who don't return, however, will find limited opportunities throughout their lives. They will always be struggling to catch up. Their dreams might be deferred for a lifetime.

4

Helping Teens Stay in School

MOST DROPOUTS ADVISE fellow teens to stay in school. "Find a role model," says one dropout who returned. "Could be your best friend, could be anybody. Find something to believe in or find someone that understands you."[61] Sometimes it is not easy to find help and support, but they are available. Schools, families, and communities today are all working to help teens stay in school.

Support from families

Parents play a key role in preventing students from dropping out. Studies show that a student's success in school is directly related to family support and expectations. Students are more likely to graduate when parents have high expectations, including that they remain in school. Comments from teens themselves show this to be true:

> I have not dropped out of school because of my father. Before he died, he told me how proud he would be when my diploma is hanging on the wall beside his. Now he'll never see my diploma, but I know when I get it, it will be something like granting his final wish.

> I guess the most important thing that caused me not to drop out of high school was my family. They helped me with my teachers and were patient. I wasn't forced to be the best in the class, but my parents just asked me to do my best.[62]

When the community—including the teen's friends and their families—also values education, most obstacles to

A supportive family is an important part of success for many young people in school.

completing school can be overcome. Social worker Beth Rosenthal saw this when she studied a Haitian community of about twenty thousand people in the New York City area. "The study focused on Haitians because they fit the profile of school leavers: they are poor, black, and live in households with high levels of stress," she writes in an article for *Social Work in Education*. Some of this stress included "interpersonal conflict and physical abuse."[63] Yet despite these risk factors, almost all of the students graduated from high school. What made the difference?

Rosenthal reports that nearly all young people interviewed said that their parents valued education and expected them to graduate. "In interview after interview," she says, "the youths indicated that they were highly aware of their parents' expectation for education, that they were obedient and respectful of their parents' wishes, and that they and their friends valued education highly."[64]

For example, one teen told Rosenthal, "My parents are always giving us lectures about how important education is. They have a sense of pride—you go to school. Haitian parents would kill themselves to send you to school." Another teen expressed the same sentiments when talking about his parents and education. "They would not let me drop out,"[65] he said.

Community support goes hand in hand with family support. Most families in the Haitian community Rosenthal studied shared the same views about the importance of education. As a result, even the peer pressure was positive. One young man stated that most of his friends are in college and he intends to follow. Another student found support not only from her mother—who wanted her to complete college as well as high school—but from her boyfriend, too. "He pushes me . . . when I'm down, he always finds a way to reason it out."[66]

When families can't help

Most families, even those in trouble, want their children to succeed in school. The majority of dropouts report that their families didn't want them to leave. In the Department of Education study that followed one class of students, three-quarters of teens said their parents tried to talk them into staying, and two-thirds said their parents were upset with their decision to leave. Only one-fifth of parents said it was OK to leave.

But not all parents are willing or able to give the support their teens need to stay in school. They may be too tired at the end of the day to argue with their teen about homework. Or they may not understand the school's requirements for graduation or even for day-to-day performance.

Other families have overwhelming problems— unemployment, alcohol or drug addiction, medical problems, financial uncertainty—that leave little or no time to pay attention to their children. Teens in such homes have a high risk of dropping out, especially if their friends are also from troubled homes. In these cases, schools and communities must offer the help and support that's needed.

Caring teachers and other adults

Teachers are probably second only to parents in helping teens stay in school. Just as dropouts often say that "no one cared," most at-risk students who stay in school talk about a special teacher or coach who cared about them. One survey asked teens what school personnel did that helped

Many students feel that having thoughtful and caring teachers has prevented them from dropping out of school.

them stay in school. The top answers were: "Listened to my problems . . . showed concern . . . helped me like myself . . . expected me to succeed . . . [was] patient and understanding . . . showed respect . . . [and] helped with problems."[67] Other students have said:

> The reason that I did not drop out of high school is because I had very nice teachers that helped me with my work when I needed help.

> I had teachers who pushed me to do everything I could to pass my courses.

> I had the best track coach and I could trust him.

> One of my teachers who was very caring told me not to drop out of high school.[68]

The adult doesn't have to be a teacher. He or she can be a coach, a principal, a guidance counselor, an aide, even someone from the community—anyone who believes in the student and offers encouragement and help. Such a person is called a mentor. Some high schools today are setting up formal mentoring programs to help students stay in school.

Getting help from mentors

"At-risk students don't have an advocate, someone to stand up for them,"[69] says Steve Michaels, a guidance counselor at DeLand High School in Volusia County, Florida. Yet students who are failing courses, skipping classes, and misbehaving are most in need of someone who cares. To give them that support, his school began a voluntary mentoring program in 1998. Mentors meet with their students in small groups at least once a week. They keep track of their students' progress, help them set weekly goals, and make sure they are attending classes. The mentors listen and offer advice and encouragement. Michaels explains:

> The idea of our program is not to lecture the students or hassle them, but to let them know there's an adult who's interested in them—who in a way is their friend, but at the same time is also giving them a little push. The mentor is available, too, to provide some advice or assistance on a regular basis.

Receiving extra help from adult mentors and others helps many teens achieve success in school.

What you find is that a lot of these kids don't have it in the home. Either both parents are working or they're working split shifts, or they're just not able to be there on a regular basis to check on their kids. The kid'll go home and say, "Yeah, everything's fine, my homework's done." And the parent often doesn't have the time to make sure things are really fine.[70]

The mentor becomes the adult who *is* able to find the time. Miracles are not expected. Failing students don't suddenly become A students. But small successes are noted and applauded to give encouragement and to help build the self-confidence that failing students lack. Marilyn Smith, a career specialist at DeLand High, states, "This is not something that can be done overnight. The students' problems have accumulated over a long period of time. So basically, what we're trying to do is make sure the self-esteem is there, because that's a big part of it. We're also trying to build trust. That's where we start."[71]

Smith is a mentor to seven students—five boys and two girls. They all have academic problems. Their collective grade point average is 1.7, slightly under a C average. Some have family problems that keep them from focusing on school. Others need jobs to help their families. Some find it hard to concentrate during class, or they find the work difficult, and then fall behind and just give up. Smith tries to help her students see that education is important. She works to help them succeed. "I tell them that they can be successful no matter what happens outside of school, no matter what happens at home,"[72] she says. She talks with their teachers, finds them tutors, and listens to what they say.

Success and positive experiences

Her students are making some progress. One student, Bob, had been in trouble both in school and outside of school. He was failing almost all of his courses when he entered the mentoring program. Like many of Smith's students, he said that his classes were boring. Today, he says that he stayed in school "because of Mrs. Smith. If you have a problem with your teachers, she'll talk to them. It's not just an empty promise. She does it." He adds, "She sends us cards for encouragement. She doesn't let us quit."[73] Smith has also found jobs for Bob, giving him responsibility and a chance to earn some money. All of this is important in building confidence.

Another student, Susan, is still a freshman at age seventeen. She moved to DeLand from southern Florida, where she had been in and out of school for several years. Smith is trying to help Susan graduate in three years. Susan admits that before she became involved with the mentoring program, she wasn't trying. She cut classes and didn't hand in assignments. "Mrs. Smith has been there for all of us," she says. "She actually cares. I was failing English and she talked to the teacher. The teacher let me make up my work." Susan's behavior had to change, too. "I said I'd do the work," she says, "and I'm not a person to break promises."[74] After she graduates, Susan wants to join the marines and become a registered nurse.

A highlight of the year for Smith's students was a chance to work at Sea World of Orlando over spring break. They worked as vendors selling souvenirs in the giftshops or snacks in food service. "They were so proud when I went down to see them," she says. "It meant a lot to them to have responsible jobs."[75] Positive experiences surrounding school encourage students to stay in, do well, and graduate.

National mentoring programs

Even though not all high schools have mentoring programs, teens can still find mentors in their communities. Some organizations that provide mentors are Big Brothers/Big Sisters of America, Boys Clubs/Girls Clubs, Cities in Schools, and the YMCA/YWCA. In addition, the National Mentoring Partnership, an organization based in Washington, D.C., is working throughout the country to match young people with mentors. It also teaches adults about mentoring and offers them training in how to be good mentors. The goal of the National Mentoring Partnership is to see 2 million young people in responsible mentoring relationships.

How important are mentors? President Bill Clinton has said, "People who grew up in difficult circumstances and yet are successful have one thing in common . . . at a critical junction in their early adolescence they had a positive relationship with a caring adult."[76] The research seems to agree. A 1995 study by the Big Brothers/Big Sisters of America showed that young people with mentors are less likely to begin using illegal drugs and drinking alcohol. They are also less likely to skip school and cut classes. Another study found that high school students from families receiving public assistance were more likely to graduate from high school and even go on to college if they had a

mentor. One young woman named Kathy writes about her experience with a mentor:

One-on-one study time with a mentor can help a student tremendously in school.

> I come from a broken home—my mother is in a shelter and my brother is a ward of the government. My goals are to become an accountant, to have my own accounting firm, and to bring my family back together when I'm able. . . . Negative things come up when you live in poverty, you think about maybe wanting to sell drugs to get money, but then you know it is wrong. If you do something negative, it never comes back positive. You have to be strong and be your own person. . . . If you have a problem, a mentor can help. I could have dropped out of school. I showed Rose [her mentor] that I wanted to get to college, to make a life. I'm a sophomore now at Bowie State. It's still hard. But [Rose] used her connections to help me get an internship. . . . She helps me out, gives me advice about work, and about life. A mentor can help make a bad situation better.[77]

Kathy met Rose, a businesswoman, when she interviewed her as part of a class assignment in high school. Over the three months that the interviews took place, she

Young people can seek help from family friends, coaches or counselors, or members of a church or synagogue.

asked Rose to be her mentor. The National Mentoring Partnership encourages all teens who need help with school, jobs, or personal problems to try to find a mentor. If their school doesn't have a program, they can contact an organization that provides mentors. Or they can do what Rose did—ask someone they know. It can be a friend of the family, a neighbor, someone at school, a coach or counselor at a youth group, someone at their church or synagogue, or someone where they work. Anyone a teen can trust, who believes in them and will take the time to support them, can be a mentor.

Helping teen parents

Mentors can also help pregnant girls and teen parents as they face a new and overwhelming responsibility. But teen parents need more than mentoring. They need help to stay in school and graduate, so that they will be able to make a good life for themselves and their baby—and not end up on welfare or working in dead-end, minimum-wage jobs.

Many years ago, pregnant teens were not permitted to stay in school. They had to drop out, whether they wanted to or not. But this is no longer true. Title IX of the Education Amendment Act of 1972 requires that all resources available to students must also be available to pregnant girls. Yet being permitted to remain in school is not enough. Teen mothers—and fathers, too—need special services such as child care, support groups, parenting classes, vocational counseling, and sometimes help in finding health care. Elisa is a teen mother who needed such services:

> When I realized I was pregnant I thought my life had ended. My dreams of college, of even finishing high school, were over. I was ready to drop out when I read of the Teen Parent Program. I decided to enroll, and the support I got there made all the difference.

> I only missed three weeks of school when my baby was born. My mother works, and I had no one at home to care for Travis. But my school has a child care center, so he went to school with me. I'll graduate in June, and I'm going to college to learn accounting.[78]

Programs like the one in Elisa's school are especially important today because changes in federal and state welfare laws make it harder for teen mothers to receive welfare benefits.

The majority of school districts in the United States still do not have teen parenting programs like the one that helped Elisa. But many do, and their numbers are increasing. Some offer programs in separate facilities, but more and more districts are developing programs at their regular high schools, often with state funding. They are making this effort because they know that teen parents who drop out of school are going to be less prepared to take care of themselves and their babies than those who complete their education.

A teen parent program in action

In Florida, school districts are required by the state to help teen parents remain in school. Since 1986 the state has "guaranteed pregnant and parenting teens that, if they wanted to continue to earn their high school diploma, they could receive child care services, transportation, and health and social services within the school system," says Ginger Masingill, director of the Teen Parent Center at Volusia County's DeLand High School. "Each school district has a lot of leeway in how they want to design these programs, but every county in Florida has some type of teen parenting education program."[79]

Volusia County offers two types of programs: A pregnant girl in high school can remain in her home school or attend a separate school for pregnant girls—the choice is hers. If she chooses to attend the separate school, she takes classes there throughout her pregnancy and the birth of her child. Then she finishes out the semester and returns to her home school. If she needs child care, she can attend one of the county's two high schools that have a Teen Parent Center.

Making a difference

The Teen Parent Center at DeLand provides on-site child care, with separate rooms for infants, crawling babies, and toddlers. Most children are three years old or younger, but the center occasionally cares for four-year-olds, too, when the mother had her baby at a very young age. All caretakers are trained in child care, and the program is developmental, which means that caretakers follow the progression of each child's development. If they notice delays or problems with language development or walking, for example, they will see that the child receives the proper care.

The teen mothers drop off their babies at the center in the morning, but return later for a daily ninety-minute parenting class. Child care supervisor Cindy Appleby says,

> The parenting school is a laboratory school, a hands-on classroom. We're actually doing parenting here with the babies, and the young mothers can see it and do it. . . . Some days it's a classroom setting. Some days, because of a crisis, we will model and talk about what to do. Everybody is very individual. Sometimes tears need to be taken care of. Young moms need help.[80]

Academics are stressed, too, because the program's mission is to try to make sure these young mothers graduate from school. Sometimes Masingill tutors failing students. Other times she discusses behavior problems with the discipline deans. In an interview with the authors of *Books, Babies, and School-Age Parents* she says that

> [school officials] are with me as long as we work out a way to make the students accountable. When our students are absent, the attendance clerks call me. If the baby has a temp of 102°, and the Mom has no one else to take care of him, I tell them. I also see that she gets assignments from her teachers.[81]

For many students, the Teen Parent Center makes the difference between going to school and dropping out. One young mother, feeding her fourteen-month-old son, says, "My dad was going to take me out of school and home school me because I didn't have a baby sitter . . . and I didn't want that."[82] She is now a senior, a straight-A student, and plans to attend community college next year.

Teen parent centers at high schools are an easy way for teen mothers to receive care for their children while they focus on getting an education.

Fathers are not forgotten in teen parent programs. At DeLand, some attend the parenting class to spend time with their babies. Other programs offer support groups for fathers. "A lot of times I feel I can't make it anymore," says one sixteen-year-old father. "I need support. I don't get it at home much, but I do get support in the teen fathers group. It helps knowing I'm not the only teen dad. It makes me feel a lot better."[83] Experts believe that programs for teen fathers help them stay in school and better handle their responsibilities as fathers.

Other teen parent programs

Teen parent programs vary throughout the country, but all are committed to keeping young parents in school. California has funded a program called School-Age Parent Infant Development (SAPID) since 1975. Teen parents continue their education at their home school, but in addition to regular classes, they take a class in parenting and earn another credit working in the campus's child care center. The program helps students stay in school and also helps them adjust to their new role as parents.

Another program, called GRADS, was developed in Ohio and now operates in sixteen other states as well. GRADS is an in-school program designed to keep pregnant girls and teen parents in school, teach them good parenting skills, and prepare them for work and for the challenges of balancing work and family. GRADS teachers not only teach special classes, but they also have individual student conferences, visit students at home and in the hospital, and work with social service agencies and health care providers. All of this support offers teen parents many alternatives to dropping out of school.

Making school more relevant

In addition to helping teen parents, schools today are starting to pay more attention to those students who are not planning to attend college. Most dropouts were students who didn't see college in their futures. They saw no relationship between their courses and a future job and they were often correct. U.S. high schools place most of their emphasis on preparing students for college. Vocational training has not received the resources and the respect that academic courses do. Yet such programs do exist and are beginning to receive more funding. In 1994, President Clinton signed the School-to-Work Opportunities Act, which provides federal money for states to create programs that prepare students for high-wage, high-skill jobs. Knowing that their schooling can lead to a good job is an incentive for teens to stay in school.

Volusia County, Florida, was one of many counties to apply for a federal grant. One program that it developed is called Career Connection. Students begin thinking about careers as early as middle school. In-depth exploration begins in ninth grade, as students learn about the following "Career Clusters": agriscience and natural resources, communications and the arts, business and marketing, engineering and manufacturing, and health and human

Many high school dropouts feel the education they receive will not serve them in the future. Therefore new education programs geared toward training teens for future jobs are becoming more common.

services. Students learn what careers are available in their area of interest and what training and education are needed. Career specialist Marilyn Smith says,

> We build a little each year. At DeLand High, for example, ninth graders fill out interest inventories, listen to guest speakers, and take small-group field trips. As they move through school, they can take specific courses in their cluster. By senior year, they're researching colleges, interviewing local business people, and job shadowing.[84]

In job shadowing, students go to a business and "shadow," or follow, someone as they do their job. The goal of the Career Connection program is to keep students focused on their reason for being in school.

Vocational programs

A regional vocational-technical school is another way for high school students to prepare for a career. One example is Penta County Vocational School in Perrysburg, Ohio, which draws students from sixteen school districts in five local counties. They receive training for a future career in one of six major areas: arts and communications; business and management; construction, transportation, and manufacturing; environment and agriculture; health; and public service. They also take high school courses in math, science, and English. When students receive their high school diploma, they are ready to enter the workplace.

Students specializing in Business Computer Tech Prep, for example, receive A+ certification in the repair of computer equipment as well as certification in other aspects of computer technology. Those majoring in automotive technology leave school skilled in all areas of automobile repair. Clerical specialists get hands-on office training in offices within the school. Those students in the cosmetology program become eligible to take the state licensing exams. The culinary arts program includes instruction and experience in a school-operated restaurant. The list goes on, but the important point is that all of these students graduate from high school with the skills to find a good job and will have opportunities to advance.

Some regular high schools have programs where students take their academic courses for half of the day and then work or take classes elsewhere for the other half. Larger schools might have vocational programs right on the school campus. The Volusia County School District in Florida has set up vocational academies within its regular high schools. One such academy at Deltona High School is a three-year program for teens who want to go into drafting, architecture, printing, and carpentry. "This academy is trying to appeal to those kids who may not be college bound, but are looking to learn a skill so that they can get a job right out of high school,"[85] says principal Mike Schilsky.

Vocational programs that train teens in areas such as computer technology help prepare students to enter the workplace.

Service learning

Another way some schools try to make school more relevant is through service learning. Service learning is a way of including community service as part of the curriculum. Marty Duckenfield, public information director of the National Dropout Prevention Center, writes:

> Students who drop out of school tend to be youth who are alienated from their schools and communities. They lack the healthy connections that successful children have enjoyed over the years. [They] do not participate in school activities; they do not join school or community organizations. . . . Service learning can provide the sense of belonging that is so desperately needed by adolescents. Working with a team of classmates on a meaningful activity where a real difference is being made in the community can have enormous impact. Solving problems with peers can bond these students together and provide the support base so needed by these young people.[86]

One example of community service is for a student to tutor a younger child. Research has shown that both are helped. The younger child not only improves academically, but self-esteem goes up with having an older "friend." The tutors also benefit. By teaching something, they learn it better themselves. In addition, by helping someone else, they feel better about themselves. This kind of experience is a plus for all teens. For the teen who has often felt like a failure, it can be even more important.

There are many other ways to serve. In Kentucky, programs receiving the state's Learn and Serve funds were invited to display their projects at the 1997 state fair. The displays showed a variety of projects. *Learning & Serving: The Southern Service Learning Newsletter* reports:

> The energy and enthusiasm of the students were seen in such displays as a fourth grade intergenerational literacy project, a fifth grade tornado safety campaign, a middle school community beautification project, and a high school bicycle repair service for young children. The students took great pride in sharing information on their project with fair-goers.[87]

The newsletter reported on another service-learning project in Troy, Alabama, where art students at Charles Henderson High School painted a mural on a one-hundred-foot-long wall on the side of the Troy Citizen building. The mural, part of a project to revitalize the downtown, traces the history of Troy and the county. When students feel part

Teenage boys deliver groceries to an elderly woman. Encouraging learning through community service is another way schools try to promote a connection between school and the real world.

of something, they feel better about themselves, and are less likely to give up on their futures.

"Teachers listen"

Approximately 80 percent of new jobs in the next decade will require some training beyond high school. Dropouts will become even more disadvantaged. But even troubled teens don't have to drop out. There is always a way to stay in school, as one dropout discovered when she returned to school. "Teachers listen," she says, "even if you don't think they did." She received help from her parents and the principal, and in the end, she says proudly, "I passed every class." [88]

5

Getting a
Second Chance

Despite ALL THE prevention programs, approximately half a million teens still drop out of school each year. Do they have to join the millions of dropouts locked into low-paying jobs, with a future of "dreams deferred"? Not according to U.S. Secretary of Education Richard W. Riley:

> Alternative programs that give young people a second chance are a growing phenomena. . . . Young people at risk shouldn't just be left on their own to hang out on the street. New attention needs to be paid to finding ways to encourage many more dropouts to drop back in to school, so that they have a real chance of living a decent life. When young people drop out they do more than just give up their education, they are too often giving up on themselves.[89]

Many school systems, government agencies, community colleges, and even private companies are answering Riley's challenge. Alternative schools and programs are available throughout the country. The most popular alternative route to a high school diploma is to receive GED certification, also called a high school equivalency diploma. In fact, in 1995, about one-sixth of all high school diplomas issued were GED equivalency diplomas.

What is the GED?

The GED is the common term for the General Education Development Tests. These tests were first developed for the U.S. Army during World War II when the federal gov-

ernment wanted to help veterans obtain a college education. But many veterans didn't even have a high school diploma. In 1942 the GED tests were developed to see if they had the knowledge and ability to go to college. From the beginning, there were five tests covering five subject areas: reading, writing, math, science, and social studies. At first, they were used mainly for determining college admissions. After the war, however, nonveterans started taking the tests, too, and states awarded high school credentials to those who passed.

The number of tests and basic multiple-choice format of the GED tests have remained the same over the years. The content has changed, however, to reflect changes in curriculum, and the writing of a short essay was added in 1988. The tests have also become more challenging to

GED tests, developed to help World War II veterans who were unable to complete their high school education, offer teenagers a way to receive high school credentials.

Classes like this résumé writing class supply teens with the tools needed to find a job.

pass. The material is more difficult and passing standards have been raised, most recently in 1997.

The tests themselves don't measure knowledge recall. Rather, the test-taker is asked to read written passages and answer questions about them. Most of the factual knowledge needed to give the right answer can be found in the passages or in supplementary sections. In the math section, mathematical formulas are provided.

The value of the GED

Every year, about three-quarters of a million high school dropouts take the GED tests. The average age of the test-takers is twenty-five years, and about one-third are members of minority groups. Most have about ten years of schooling. Some prepare for the test by taking formal programs in high schools or community colleges, while others study on their own. Of those taking the test, half a million pass and receive a GED certificate. The GED is recognized by colleges, qualifies the recipient for student-aid programs, and classifies the recipient as a high school graduate. But is it really the equivalent of a high school diploma? Do recipients have the same success at work and in future schooling as regular high school graduates? Studies have shown that when it comes to cognitive skills, that is, basic literacy and knowledge, GED recipients perform better than other dropouts and roughly equal to regular high school graduates. But there are differences.

The military, for example, noted in the 1980s that the attrition rate for GED recipients (the number who leave) was closer to that of dropouts than graduates. The U.S. Army now has a three-level system for classifying the educational attainment of those who wish to join—high school graduates are in the first level, GED recipients in the second, and dropouts in the third.

In terms of jobs and salaries, too, GED recipients fall between regular high school graduates and dropouts. They earn more than dropouts, but most studies show that they learn less than graduates. On the plus side, recent statistics showed that over 80 percent of people with a GED were working or looking for work. For dropouts, that figure was only a little more than half.

Opening doors

The most important value of the GED is that it opens the door to further education or training. About half of all GED recipients take advantage of this opportunity. They do as well as regular graduates in vocational programs, but they are less likely to receive a two-year degree and much less likely to graduate from a four-year college. This may be because they are usually older than traditional college students and have jobs or family responsibilities. On the other hand, it may also reflect a tendency to leave a situation that becomes difficult or unpleasant. As David Boesel writes in "The Street Value of the GED Diploma,"

> The GED does not certify . . . good work habits, perseverance, and the ability to function well in organizations. A high school education, on the other hand, builds cognitive skills through academic coursework and non-cognitive skills through involvement in the process of schooling—e.g., regular attendance, meeting deadlines, demonstrating competence, and cooperating with others. A high school diploma signals the possession of both kinds of skills at certain levels.[90]

Having a GED is better than being a dropout, but it is not the same as having a regular high school diploma. While the GED does open many doors, high school dropouts may be better off with a regular diploma. If they can't succeed in their regular high school, they might look for an alternative school.

Storefront School

One such school is Storefront School, a "one-room schoolhouse" in Daytona Beach, Florida. Every day, Monday through Friday, its forty students work at computers. Half attend in the morning, half in the afternoon. On a sunny February morning, Susan is writing a term paper on careers in real estate. "I work for a condo company arranging appointments for people who are interested in buying a condo," she explains. "I'd like to work in real estate when I graduate." About eight feet away, Mike is on the Internet, exploring educational requirements for careers. "I'm looking to see what it takes to be a pilot,"[91] he says. And across the room, Kim is working on a literature assignment, getting ready to write a paper on a King Arthur story. All are feeling successful, but that wasn't always the case.

"I wasn't focused when I was in school," says Kim. "I didn't do anything in class and the teachers didn't pay attention. They gave their time to the kids who were more focused." Susan tells a similar story of not concentrating. "Some teachers tried," she explains, "but, like in Math, if I didn't get it and asked a question, it still wouldn't connect. And then the bell would ring or something."[92] She never went to ask for help.

Alternative schools that promote learning through computers can be helpful to teens who don't perform well in traditional schools.

Storefront School is different. Students work at their own pace using a software learning package called an integrated computer network. All the computer stations are networked together, and the different subjects can overlap or mix together. For example, an English lesson in reading might also cover a period of history. The programs are performance based, which means students move ahead only when they have mastered the material. A teacher is there to answer questions and help. "I love the program here," says Susan. "In the morning, I can't wait to get here to do some more."[93]

Storefront School began with a federal grant and now is funded through the public schools. Students range in age from sixteen to twenty-one, although most are between sixteen and eighteen. Students must test at the ninth grade level or better; those that test lower can receive remedial help at their high school, the local community college, or through private tutoring. Although students do their academic work individually on computers, they come together on a regular basis for peer counseling classes, where they talk about all kinds of teen issues.

Storefront School teaches more than the academic curriculum. It also teaches responsibility and the importance of following through. Attendance is mandatory. An unexcused absence is grounds for dismissal. Director Kathleen Kirkendall explains:

> I think Storefront is the last resort, where they've tried regular school, they've tried home school, private school, adult ed possibly. Maybe they've dropped out and worked for a while. When they get here, they sign a contract that says they are going to attend school every day, that they will finish their credits here. . . . It's a graduation program.
>
> They must have a part-time job for a minimum of fifteen hours and no more than thirty. They have to keep that same job the entire time they're enrolled. We're looking for stability. . . . They tend to run from situation to situation—the manager didn't like me, so I'll go to work at Burger King— instead of working out the situation or sticking it out. So that's what we're teaching them. We have one case manager whose entire job is to work with the students and their job sites.[94]

Storefront School also requires that students have definite future plans in place before they graduate—going to college, working at least thirty hours a week, going into the military, or a combination such as part-time work and part-time college. "You're a productive individual when you leave here," says Kirkendall. "You can't leave here to be a beach bum or be a couch potato."[95]

Oakland Street Academy

The Street Academy was created in 1973 by the National Urban League, the Bay Area Urban League, and the National Institute of Education in collaboration with the Oakland Unified School District. The school is currently operated by the Bay Area Urban League under contract with and funded by the local school district. From the beginning, it has helped students who weren't succeeding in a traditional high school. Its smaller size—Oakland Street Academy has only 160 students in grades nine to twelve—makes it easier for teachers to get to know their students.

That personal attention makes a huge difference. Former student Luanne talks about the regular high school that she left. "Nobody cared," she says, "nobody was in charge, I never saw the principal."[96] With seventy-two absences on one report card and fifty-five on another, she was on her way to being a dropout statistic. Then she learned about the Street Academy.

It was different there, Luanne found. The teachers were more involved. They also served as counselors. After thirty days at the school, she was able to choose a teacher to be her personal counselor. This personal counselor was available to help her with every aspect of her life, from personal

Small classes help students develop a close relationship with their teachers while getting needed personal attention.

advice to parent contact to graduation and jobs. The counselor became, in effect, her mentor. The counselor also stayed in touch with Luanne's mother, and like all personal counselors at the school, would let her know if Luanne was missing classes, not handing in homework, or having other problems.

But the Street Academy didn't make things easy for Luanne. The atmosphere was strict and students were expected to achieve. "[The teachers] showed their authority," she says. "If you wanted to act silly, they weren't babysitters." But they were encouraging:

> They taught in a positive way. Instead of acting like, "No, you don't know the answer. Oh, my." That is total humiliation. The teacher would look at what is said and try to fit it into some kind of context. Either "You're partially right" or "I might be able to understand if you could explain" as opposed to "No. Never. Wrong." It always made me feel good. The majority of the teachers had the attitude, "I can help you learn." [97]

Thomas, another former student who was failing in a regular high school, talks about his success at Street Academy: "People were there telling me I was smart, when people all my life had been telling me I was dumb. And I'd say, 'Well maybe if they think I'm smart, I'll just be smart.' It gets in there; you sort of confuse yourself psychologically." [98]

According to Kitty Kelly Epstein, professor of education, who taught at the Oakland Street Academy for several years, "The philosophy at the Academy is that the students are O.K. We tell them, 'There's nothing wrong with you. The traditional high school didn't fit you, that's all.' We teach a college prep curriculum and the kids succeed." [99]

Horizon Education Centers

The Horizon Education Centers in Orange County, California, also offer a second chance to students who have not succeeded in a traditional school environment. They are part of a dropout prevention program run by the Alternative Charter and Correctional Schools and Services Division of the county's department of education. Like the

Oakland Street Academy, the Horizon Centers emphasize small classes and counseling. However, they are not limited to high school students. The centers are open to children and teens—from kindergarten through grade twelve—who have been expelled from their regular school, who are on probation, or who need counseling to work through problems that keep them from succeeding in school.

Working closely with teachers and receiving individual attention helps many students succeed in their education.

The Horizon program began in 1983 with one site and five students. Today, the Orange County dropout program includes not only the Horizon Centers, but other educational programs as well. School sites are located where the students are—in churches, storefronts, group homes, homes for abused and neglected children, community day schools, probation partnership programs, and even lock-up facilities, such as a juvenile hall or mountain camps. Between seven and eight thousand students are served each day, and approximately six hundred graduated in 1999.

All sites are kept small. The aim is to create a trusting environment. Counseling is the key, writes Christine Gober-Huntington of the county's department of education. She says Horizon students have a variety of problems and needs. Many of them are involved in gangs, and some have been expelled from their schools of residence for bringing weapons on campus. . . . Teachers act as role models, offer guidance and often assist students with personal problems such as finding jobs. A home-like atmosphere is encouraged. [The schools also work with the county's Probation Department.] Probation officers are seen as partners who provide services to help students adjust socially and to become successful in school.

The . . . students who graduate from Horizon each year are students who have dropped out or have been asked to leave traditional schools. . . . [We] cannot afford to lose any of these students. These are our kids. We cannot throw away even one.[100]

The students themselves demonstrate the success of this belief. One former student, Eddie, spoke at a superintendents' meeting:

My street name is Rocco. I should not be here today. I should be dead. I started my first day of junior high school with a gun hidden under my coat. I was kicked out of school at 13 years old for assault and battery on another student. But I am here today because someone cared and no matter what, never gave up on me.[101]

Today even students with no behavior problems are asking to attend Horizon schools. These students, says Gober-Huntington, don't feel they fit into a traditional high school setting. They want a smaller, more homelike environment. "This should be a clear message to the traditional schools," she adds. "Schools that have become too large, too bureaucratic, and disconnected from their students will not survive. Schools that provide students with caring support, clear boundaries, and expectations will continue to grow."[102]

Community college and other programs

How can teens learn about alternative schools in their community? A good place to start is the local high school or community college, where counselors will know what is available in their area. In addition, many community colleges themselves have high school diploma programs for older teens and adults. Daytona Beach Community College in Florida, for example, offers both GED preparation and a separate program that gives an adult high school diploma to dropouts age sixteen and older. Students can attend class during the day or evening. Five teachers work with approximately three hundred students over the course of a week. Teachers act as a source of help and guidance, rather than conduct traditional classes. The program is flexible and allows students to work at their own rate, although daily attendance is required.

Other types of programs, too, are available around the country. In his article on the value of the GED, David Boesel mentions programs in Rhode Island, Tennessee, and California. Dropouts can sign an education contract to complete the traditional requirements for a high school diploma. They go to approved learning centers where experienced teachers can answer questions and provide tutoring. Students must pass tests before moving on to the next level. These programs aren't "suitable for students who have very large educational deficits, [but they seem] to work well for many who are just a year or two behind,"[103] says Boesel.

Job Corps

The federal government also offers programs to help dropouts get the training and education they need to find skilled jobs. One of these is the Job Corps, a vocational program for teens and young adults from sixteen to twenty-four. Job Corps is a residential program, and most students live at a Job Corps center during their training. There are more than one hundred centers, located in forty-four states and the District of Columbia.

Besides the age requirement, Job Corp applicants must be legal residents of the United States, have financial need, and be "ready, willing, and able to participate fully in an educational environment."[104] Job Corps has "zero tolerance" for drug and alcohol abuse, and all applicants must sign a preadmission agreement pledging to support the *Zero Tolerance for Violence* policy.

"I think Job Corps is the best program out there for economically disadvantaged youth," says Jessica Catherwood, Job Corps state coordinator for admissions in Florida. "In fact, it's the best kept secret in America." Catherwood should know. She is a Job Corps graduate herself. At fifteen, she ran away from home, and at seventeen she discovered Job Corps. "I got my GED, completed the clerical training, continued into the advanced career training program, and then went on for my four-year degree. Job Corps put me on the path."[105] Now, ten years later, she is back working at Job Corps, with two other graduates on her staff as admissions counselors.

Once accepted into a Job Corps center, students receive room and board, work clothing if needed, and health care. Recreational activities such as sports and dances are offered. Students also earn money while they're training. They get leave on weekends, and after six months, a two-week paid vacation.

Finding the way

Sholonda is about to graduate from Job Corps. She already has a job waiting for her back home. She admits that before coming to Job Corps she had lost her way. She held factory jobs, but switched jobs every few months. She also hung out with the wrong crowd, got into fights, and even wrote some bad checks. Finally, she decided to turn her life around and go back to school. "I talked to my auntie who works at the Job Corps center in Batesville, Mississippi," she says. "When she told me about all the opportunities it offered I signed up." Sholanda trained to work in medical records and a medical office. Job Corps also arranged for six weeks of work experience at a local health care center. "I was a lot different when I came to Job Corps," she says. "I was lazy and pretty stubborn. Job Corps is a maturing experience. I have changed tremendously."[106]

In addition to clerical training and health occupations, Job Corps students can learn carpentry, welding, cosmetology, computer science, heavy equipment operation, culinary arts, construction trades, and many others. Students can try out different areas before making a choice. Academic education isn't neglected either. Students study reading, writing, and basic math skills, and they can earn a GED. "Sometimes

people get started late in life, or they can't afford college or it's not for them," adds Sholanda. "Job Corps understands that, and they take time to help you learn." [107]

Many federal programs have been created to give dropouts the skills they need to achieve in the workplace.

National Guard Youth Challenge Program

Another federal program for dropouts is the National Guard Youth Challenge Program, sponsored by the National Guard. Available in sixteen states, Youth Challenge is a five-and-a-half-month residency program, with an additional year of follow-up while students work on achieving their goals in their home communities. During the follow-up time, each student is paired with a mentor who helps him or her through the year. To be eligible, a teen must be a high school dropout between the ages of sixteen and eighteen. As with the Job Corps, the teen must be drug free and meet other requirements as well.

The residency part of the program is modeled after military basic training. Students are called cadets. They wear uniforms, have haircut standards, march from place to place, and do push-ups as punishment. The purpose is to give them structure, something most of them have not experienced at home or in their regular school.

"The kids [here] are kids who have experimented with drugs, who have had negative involvement with the law. Many come from dysfunctional homes,"[108] says Capt. Guy Keys in an article in *Soldiers*. Keys is the lead counselor at the Thunderbird Youth Academy, which administers the Youth Challenge program in Pryor Creek, Oklahoma. He believes that most cadets thrive in the structured atmosphere of Youth Challenge.

Learning life skills

During these five and a half months, Youth Challenge helps teens obtain their GED. But the program doesn't stop there. It teaches life skills, such as how to balance a checkbook, fill out a tax form, and buy a car or house. Students also learn about substance abuse, sexually transmitted diseases, nutrition, child rearing, gender stereotyping, and responsible citizenship. "The GED really just becomes a piece of paper if they don't develop life skills to go along with it," says Keys. "We hope to at least put them on the right track of being a good parent, of being responsible sexually, feeling a sense of community and a sense of responsibility."[109]

Students work hard and it isn't easy. As cadet Dan Brown says, "Emotionally, you're on your own. But it helps you deal more with yourself, because you can't rely on your parents anymore, you can't rely on your close friends. You've got to figure out what needs to be done. In here, you have to learn how to deal with your problems, and we do."[110]

Christina Martindale agrees. Troubles at home caused her to drop out of school, but she got a second chance when she read a newspaper article about Youth Challenge. "The Youth Challenge Program taught me how to be independent and not rely on others," she says. "It taught me leadership skills. It also showed me that no matter how difficult the past was, the future didn't have to be the same."[111] After graduation, Martindale decided to join the Louisiana Na-

Graduating from high school is an accomplishment to be proud of and opens the door to future success.

tional Guard. She became a private first class and was named the Louisiana Army Guard's Soldier of the Year.

Why defer a dream?

Teens don't have to defer their dreams. Even those who have dropped out can have a second chance. They can listen to other teens who have turned their lives around and decide to achieve that high school diploma. "It's been a long hard road getting to where I am now, and there will still be some more hard times ahead," says one former dropout. "But I reached someplace I never thought I'd be. I'm in college now." Adds another, "Anyone can do what they want if they put their mind to it."[112]

Appendix

Strategies for Staying in School

Staying in school is the smart thing to do but your problems—either at home or in school—won't go away just because you want them to. You have to figure out how to turn things around so that you *can* stay in school. Here are some suggestions from teachers, counselors, and former dropouts themselves.

Ask for help

This is probably the key. If you have serious personal problems, such as abusive or drug-addicted parents, try to find someone in your family that you can trust. If there is no one, talk to a guidance counselor, favorite teacher, or a minister or rabbi. If you are a victim of physical or sexual abuse, *tell someone immediately*. Guidance counselors and clergy will know whom to contact in social services. No one should live in a dangerous situation. And there are some things teenagers cannot—and should not—handle alone.

If your problems with your parents are less serious, talk to them about your differences when you are not upset. If you have arguments over homework or curfews, try to show them that you are responsible. You can also ask a grandparent, aunt, uncle, or someone at school, to help you approach your parents.

If your biggest problem is schoolwork, you can get help with that, too. Most teachers are willing to give extra time to students after school. Remember that teachers are people, too, and they are usually teaching a subject they love. They are glad to see students show an interest. Give them a chance. Some schools also offer courses in how to study. These courses can give you tips on how to read more effectively, how to take notes, and how to take tests. Some books can help you, too. Ask your school or town librarian for suggestions.

Join a support group

Maybe your parents just aren't going to be there for you. But you can still get help from your peers. Some schools have support groups of students who help each other stay on track. One support group in Colorado has a bulletin board on which students place stars with each other's achievements. It feels good to be recognized.

Look ahead

Try to set some long-term goals for yourself. What are your interests? What are your dreams? If there were no obstacles, what would you like to do with your life? Then ask yourself how your decisions today will affect those dreams. For example, if you'd like to be a nurse, manage a hotel, or work in an office, you need a high school diploma. Your decision to cut class or skip school will put your goal further away. Do you want that?

Set small, attainable goals

It is hard sometimes to stay focused on a long-term goal, so many people also set small goals for themselves. If you failed English, for example, decide to pass the course next semester. Even a D is passing. Or try to raise your grade in just one course, maybe from a D to a C, or from a C to a B. Achieving one goal will make you feel good about yourself. Then you can set another goal.

Join one school activity

Teens who participate in school activities feel a part of the school and are less likely to drop out. They can also make friends with other teens who have the same interests. Maybe you can't afford a musical instrument, but it doesn't cost money to sing in a chorus. If you like art, take an art class and then work on an art project around the school. Or you could go out for a school team. If you belong to a minority group, your school may have a club for students who share your ethnic background. Being with others of the same background can help you learn more about your heritage and feel more pride in yourself. Some groups learn about their culture's history and then celebrate holidays with music and daning. No matter what you like to do, finding something fun to do in school can help overcome the things you don't like.

Explore vocational education

High schools today place a lot of emphasis on college preparation. But maybe you really don't like to study and don't want to go to college. While many well-paying careers today do not require a college degree, they do require technical skills. Find out what kind of vocational or technical training your school district offers, or if there are any work/study programs. Your guidance counselor can help you.

Resist peer pressure to drop out

This is probably the hardest thing to do. If your friends are cutting classes or dropping out, it's easy to join them. But look at what they are doing. Are they just hanging around? Or are they working? If they are working, what kinds of jobs do they have? Is that what you want for yourself now—and in five or ten years? If it is hard to succeed in a class where your friends are failing, see if you can be placed in another class. Remember, your goal is to graduate.

Find a mentor

Some schools have mentoring programs. Others can help you find someone in the community, or you can call the National Mentoring Partnership (see Organizations to Contact) for suggestions. Being with someone who believes in you will help you believe in yourself, too. And studies show that teens with mentors are less likely to drop out of school.

Keep focused on the goal of graduation

You want that diploma. Make sure you know what courses are required and make sure you pass them. You don't have to get an A. Any passing grade will do. Set up a checklist for yourself and check off your accomplishments. Every check will bring you closer to your goal. Find out about any state proficiency exams. Ask if your school offers special classes to help students prepare. If so, take them. Your hard work will be rewarded when you walk across the stage at graduation and receive your high school diploma.

Notes

Introduction

1. Quoted in Richard J. Coley, *Dreams Deferred: High School Dropouts in the United States.* Policy Information Report. Princeton, NJ: Educational Testing Service, 1995, p. 2.

2. ETS Research, "Dreams Deferred: High School Dropouts Face Bleak Future," June 2, 1995. www.ets.org/research/pic/pr/dropouts.html.

3. Quoted in Edwin Farrell, *Hanging In and Dropping Out: Voices of At-Risk High School Students.* New York: Teachers College Press, Columbia University, 1990, p. 91.

4. Quoted in Farrell, *Hanging In and Dropping Out,* p. 91.

5. Quoted in Kitty Kelly Epstein, "Case Studies in Dropping Out and Dropping Back In," *Journal of Education,* vol. 174, no. 3, 1992, pp. 55+.

6. Quoted in ETS Research, "Dreams Deferred."

Chapter 1: Who Drops Out of School?

7. Quoted in *"I Dropped Out. But I Didn't Think It Would Be Like This."* Distributed by Cambridge Research Group, Charleston, WV, 1989. Videocassette.

8. Quoted in *"I Dropped Out. But I Didn't Think It Would Be Like This."*

9. Quoted in *"I Dropped Out. But I Didn't Think It Would Be Like This."*

10. Harriett D. Romo and Toni Falbo, *Latino High School Graduation: Defying the Odds.* Austin: University of Texas Press, 1996, p. 19.

11. Quoted in *"I Dropped Out. But I Didn't Think It Would Be Like This."*

12. Romo and Falbo, *Latino High School Graduation,* p. 10.

13. Will J. Jordan, Julia Lara, and James M. McPartland, "Exploring the Causes of Early Dropout Among Race-Ethnic and Gender Groups," *Youth & Society*, September 1996, pp. 62+.

14. U.S. Department of Education, Office of Educational Research and Improvement (OERI), "Defining Dropouts: A Statistical Portrait," *Reaching the Goals: Goal 2—High School Completion*, March 1994. www.ed.gov/pubs/Reaching Goals/Goal_2/Dropouts.html.

15. Yolanda G. Martinez and Ann Cranston-Gingras, "Migrant Farmworker Students and the Educational Process: Barriers to High School Completion," *High School Journal*, October 1, 1996, pp. 28+.

16. William Lowe Boyd, "What Makes Ghetto Schools Succeed or Fail?" *Teachers College Record*, Spring 1991, pp. 331+.

17. Quoted in Boyd, "What Makes Ghetto Schools Succeed or Fail?"

18. Quoted in Boyd, "What Makes Ghetto Schools Succeed or Fail?"

19. Quoted in Boyd, "What Makes Ghetto Schools Succeed or Fail?"

20. Quoted in Boyd, "What Makes Ghetto Schools Succeed or Fail?"

Chapter 2: Why Teens Drop Out

21. Quoted in *Dropout Prevention: Nowhere to Go*, distributed by AGC/United Learning, Evanston, IL, 1991, videocassette.

22. Quoted in Annie S. Barnes, *Retention of African-American Males in High School: A Study of African-American Male High School Dropouts, African-American Male Seniors, and White Male Seniors*. Lanham, MD: University Press of America, 1992, p. 77.

23. Quoted in Barnes, *Retention of African-American Males in High School*, p. 75.

24. Storefront School student, personal interview by the author, Storefront School, Daytona Beach, FL, February 10, 1999.

25. Quoted in *"I Dropped Out. But I Didn't Think It Would Be Like This."*

26. Quoted in *"I Dropped Out. But I Didn't Think It Would Be Like This."*

27. Coley, *Dreams Deferred*, p. 17.

28. Coley, *Dreams Deferred*, p. 17.

29. Romo and Falbo, *Latino High School Graduation*, p. 159.

30. Quoted in *Dropout Prevention: Nowhere to Go.*

31. Kitty Kelly Epstein, telephone interview by the author, March 24, 1999.

32. Epstein, "Case Studies in Dropping Out and Dropping Back In."

33. Quoted in Epstein, "Case Studies in Dropping Out and Dropping Back In."

34. Quoted in Romo and Falbo, *Latino High School Graduation*, p. 160.

35. Quoted in Farrell, *Hanging In and Dropping Out*, p. 106.

36. Farrell, *Hanging In and Dropping Out*, p. 114.

37. Farrell, *Hanging In and Dropping Out*, p. 96.

38. Quoted in *The News-Times*, "High School Dropouts Highest Among Minority Groups," June 23, 1997. www.newstimes.com/archive97/jun2397/rgf.htm.

39. Quoted in Susan Headden, "The Hispanic Dropout Mystery," *U.S. News & World Report*, October 20, 1997, pp.64+.

40. Joy G. Dryfoos, *Full-Service Schools: A Revolution in Health and Social Services for Children, Youth, and Families*. San Francisco: Jossey-Bass, 1994, p. 3.

41. Cyndi Terry, telephone interview by the author, March 25, 1999.

42. Quoted in Romo and Falbo, *Latino High School Graduation*, p. 132.

43. Romo and Falbo, *Latino High School Graduation*, p. 64.

44. Farrell, *Hanging In and Dropping Out*, p. 93.

45. Romo and Falbo, *Latino High School Graduation*, p. 42.

Chapter 3: Life After Dropping Out

46. Quoted in *Dropout Prevention: Nowhere to Go.*

47. Farrell, *Hanging In and Dropping Out*, p. 18.

48. *Economist*, "Virtual Jobs in Motown," March 26, 1994, p. 76.

49. Farrell, *Hanging In and Dropping Out*, p. 20.

50. Quoted in *Dropout Prevention: Nowhere to Go*

51. Quoted in *Dropout Prevention: Nowhere to Go.*

52. Quoted in *"I Dropped Out. But I Didn't Think It Would Be Like This."*

53. Quoted in *"I Dropped Out. But I Didn't Think It Would Be Like This."*

54. Quoted in *"I Dropped Out. But I Didn't Think It Would Be Like This."*

55. Quoted in *"I Dropped Out. But I Didn't Think It Would Be Like This."*

56. Quoted in *The Merrow Report*, PBS documentary, "Lost in Translation: Latinos, Schools and Society," October 4, 1998.

57. Quoted in *Dropout Prevention: Nowhere to Go.*

58. Coley, *Dreams Deferred*, p. 25.

59. National Dropout Prevention Center, "Chances of Becoming a Professional NBA Basketball Player," fact sheet, Clemson University, Clemson, SC.

60. Coley, *Dreams Deferred*, p. 27.

Chapter 4: Helping Teens Stay in School

61. Quoted in *Dropout Prevention: Nowhere to Go.*

62. Quoted in Barnes, *Retention of African-American Males in High School*, p.104.

63. Beth Spenciner Rosenthal, DSW, ACSW, "The Influence of Social Support on School Completion Among Haitians," *Social Work in Education*, January 1995, pp. 30+.

64. Rosenthal, "The Influence of Social Support on School Completion Among Haitians."

65. Quoted in Rosenthal, "The Influence of Social Support on School Completion Among Haitians."

66. Quoted in Rosenthal, "The Influence of Social Support on School Completion Among Haitians."

67. Hunter Downing, Otis LoVette, and Peter Emerson, "An Investigation of At-Risk Students' Reasons for Staying in School," *Journal of Humanistic Education and Development*, December 1994, pp. 83+.

68. Quoted in Barnes, *Retention of African-American Males in High School*, pp.108–109.

69. Steve Michaels, guidance counselor, personal interview by the author, DeLand High School, DeLand, FL, January 7, 1999.

70. Michaels, interview, January 7, 1999.

71. Marilyn Smith, career specialist, personal interview by the author, DeLand High School, DeLand, FL, January 7, 1999.

72. Smith, interview, March 17, 1999.

73. DeLand High School student, personal interview by the author, DeLand, FL, March 17, 1999.

74. DeLand High School student, interview, March 17, 1999.

75. Marilyn Smith, telephone interview by the author, July 11, 1999.

76. Quoted in National Mentoring Partnership, "About Mentoring." www.mentoring.org/mentoring.html.

77. Quoted in National Mentoring Partnership, "Find a Mentor." www.mentoring.org/youth.html.

78. Quoted in Jeanne Warren Lindsay and Sharon Githens Enright, *Books, Babies, and School-Age Parents: How to Teach Pregnant and Parenting Teens to Succeed*. Buena Park, CA: Morning Glory Press, 1997, p. 21.

79. Ginger Masingill, director, Teen Parent Center, personal interview by the author, DeLand High School, DeLand, FL, March 3, 1999.

80. Cindy Appleby, child care supervisor, Teen Parent Center, personal interview by the author, DeLand High School, DeLand, FL, March 3, 1999.

81. Quoted in Lindsay and Enright, *Books, Babies, and School-Age Parents*, pp. 210–11.

82. Student, Teen Parent Center, personal interview by the author, DeLand High School, DeLand, FL, March 3, 1999.

83. Quoted in Lindsay and Enright, *Books, Babies, and School-Age Parents*, p. 28.

84. Smith, interview, July 11, 1999.

85. Quoted in Lori Horvitz, "Tech Academy Is Hot Off Presses," *Orlando Sentinel*, March 6, 1999, p. D1.

86. Marty Duckenfield, "Service Learning: Real Dropout Prevention," National Dropout Prevention Center. www.dropoutprevention.org/effstrat/goopre.htm.

87. *Learning & Serving: The Southern Service Learning Newsletter*, "Kentucky Learn and Serve Goes to the State Fair!" Fall 1997. www.dropoutprevention.org/effstrat/S&LNews.htm.

88. Quoted in *Dropout Prevention: Nowhere to Go.*

Chapter 5: Getting a Second Chance

89. Quoted in David Thomas, "Dropout Rates Remain Stable over Last Decade," NCES press release, December 17, 1997. http://nces.ed.gov/Pressrelease/dropout.html.

90. David Boesel, "The Street Value of the GED Diploma," *Phi Delta Kappan*, September 1, 1998, pp. 65+.

91. Storefront School students, personal interviews by the author, Storefront School, Daytona Beach, FL, February 10, 1999.

92. Storefront School students, interviews, February 10, 1999.

93. Storefront School student, interview, February 10, 1999.

94. Kathleen Kirkendall, director, personal interview by the author, Storefront School, Daytona Beach, FL, February 10, 1999.

95. Kirkendall, interview, February 10, 1999.

96. Quoted in Epstein, "Case Studies in Dropping Out and Dropping Back In."

97. Quoted in Epstein, "Case Studies in Dropping Out and Dropping Back In."

98. Quoted in Epstein, "Case Studies in Dropping Out and Dropping Back In."

99. Epstein, interview, March 24, 1999.

100. Christine Gober-Huntington, "A Brighter Horizon," *Thrust for Educational Leadership*, November/December 1995, pp. 10+.

101. Quoted in Gober-Huntington, "A Brighter Horizon."

102. Christine Gober-Huntington, e-mail to author, June 4, 1999.

103. Boesel, "The Street Value of the GED Diploma."

104. Job Corps, *Success Lasts a Lifetime* (brochure).

105. Jessica Catherwood, Job Corps state coordinator for admissions, Florida, telephone interview by the author, June 7, 1999.

106. Quoted in Job Corps, *Listen Up*, "Three Amigas," Winter 1999, pp. 6, 8.

107. Quoted in Job Corps, *Listen Up*, p. 8.

108. Quoted in SFC Douglas Ide, "Challenging At-Risk Youth," *Soldiers*, November 1994. www.dtic.mil/soldiers/nov94/p42.html.

109. Quoted in Ide, "Challenging At-Risk Youth."

110. Quoted in Ide, "Challenging At-Risk Youth."

111. Quoted in Maj. Maria L. LoVasco, "Another Challenge," *On Guard*, April 1997. www.ngb.dtic.mil/grdnews/onguard/1997/apr/challeng.htm.

112. Quoted in *Dropout Prevention: Nowhere to Go.*

Organizations to Contact

Job Corps
National Office of Job Corps
U.S. Department of Labor
Employment and Training Administration
200 Constitution Ave. NW
Washington, DC 20210
(800) 733-JOBS
website: www.jobcorps.org

Job Corps is a national job training program created in 1964 to give young men and women between the ages of sixteen and twenty-four a fresh start. It is a residential program with centers in forty-four states and the District of Columbia. It provides the skills students need to get good jobs in a wide variety of occupations and also offers students the opportunity to earn a GED certificate. Students receive a living allowance, and when they complete the program, they are given a readjustment allowance (based on the amount of time they spent at Job Corps) to help them when they leave the program. The Job Corps website provides information about the program and links to specific state programs.

National Dropout Prevention Center/Network
Clemson University
209 Martin St.
Clemson, SC 29634-5111
(864) 656-2599
fax: (864) 656-0136

website: www.dropoutprevention.org
e-mail: ndpc@clemson.edu

The National Dropout Prevention Center/Network was established in 1986 at Clemson University. Its national membership includes more than fifteen hundred professionals in education, business, psychology, social work, and other areas. The center/network serves as a nationwide clearinghouse for programs, organizations, and resource materials on dropout prevention. Much of its information, including a database of resources, can be accessed online at its website.

National Guard Youth Challenge Program
Office of Public Affairs and Community Support
1411 Jefferson Davis Highway, Suite 11200
Arlington, VA 22202-3231
(703) 607-2664
fax: (703) 607-1744
website: www.mentoring.org/programs/nationalguardy_r_s.html
e-mail: padillaj@ngb.ang.af.mil

The National Guard Youth Challenge Program provides education, self-discipline, job skills, and values training for high school dropouts, age sixteen to eighteen, who are drug free and not in trouble with the law. It involves a military-style residential phase, followed by a year of continued support and mentoring in the corpsmember's community. In some programs, corps members earn a financial stipend at graduation.

National Mentoring Partnership
1400 I St. NW, Suite 850
Washington, DC 20005
(202) 729-4345
fax: (202) 729-4341
website: www.mentoring.org/aboutus.html

The National Mentoring Partnership promotes the idea of responsible adults acting as mentors for young people. The program works with educators, clergy, corporate and community leaders, elected officials, and youth development and mentoring experts to provide ways for adults and children to connect in a mentoring relationship. It is also a resource for mentors and mentoring programs and develops training programs for mentors. Its website contains links to information about mentoring, as well as links to state organizations and to organizations providing mentors.

Suggestions for Further Reading

Duane Brown, *Dropping Out or Hanging In: What You Should Know Before Dropping Out of School*. Chicago: VMG Career Horizons, NTC/Contemporary Publishing Group, 1998. Gives facts about dropping out of school, and then, using workbook format, helps teens look at who they are, what they value, how they make decisions, and what their long-term goals are.

Debra Goldentyer, *Dropping Out of School*. Austin, TX: Raintree Steck-Vaughn, 1994. Using interviews and case studies, discusses the consequences of dropping out and offers encouraging tips on staying in school and getting back in if a teen has already left.

Gail B. Stewart, *The Other America: Teen Dropouts*. San Diego, CA: Lucent Books, 1999. Explores the lives of four dropouts, showing what led to their dropping out of school and what they are doing now.

Claudine G. Wirths and Mary Bowman-Kruhm, *I Hate School: How to Hang In and When to Drop Out*. New York: Thomas Y. Crowell, 1987. Offers straightforward advice on how teens can better manage their lives to succeed in school and where to turn if they have serious family or personal problems. Also gives tips on studying, homework, and other aspects of schoolwork.

Works Consulted

Books

Annie S. Barnes, *Retention of African-American Males in High School: A Study of African-American Male High School Dropouts, African-American Male Seniors, and White Male Seniors*. Lanham, MD: University Press of America, 1992. Presents the results of a study on why African-American males drop out of high school, compares the dropouts with those who stay in, and makes recommendations to schools and families to help these young men stay in school.

Joy G. Dryfoos, *Full-Service Schools: A Revolution in Health and Social Services for Children, Youth, and Families*. San Francisco: Jossey-Bass, 1994. Discusses the idea of schools being the center for social services—health, mental health, family service, recreation, and culture—as well as education.

Edwin Farrell, *Hanging In and Dropping Out: Voices of At-Risk High School Students*. New York: Teachers College Press, Columbia University, 1990. Discusses the quest of all adolescents to discover who they are and where they fit in. Presents interviews with young people in New York City who, for many reasons, are not finding the answers in their high schools.

Jeanne Warren Lindsay and Sharon Githens Enright, *Books, Babies, and School-Age Parents: How to Teach Pregnant and Parenting Teens to Succeed*. Buena Park, CA: Morning Glory Press, 1997. Discusses successful teen parent programs and offers advice on how to set up such a program.

Harriett D. Romo and Toni Falbo, *Latino High School Graduation: Defying the Odds*. Austin: University of Texas

Press, 1996. Using case histories, this book explores the problems Latino teens face in high school and offers suggestions on how schools can help increase the number of graduates.

U.S. Bureau of the Census, *Statistical Abstract of the United States: 1997*. 117th ed. Washington, DC: GPO, 1997. Provides tables and statistics on social, political, and economic aspects of American life.

Periodicals, Reports, Brochures, TV Documentaries, Videos

Alcoholism & Drug Abuse Weekly, "Health Risk Behavior Is High Among Dropouts, Who Have Little Access to Services, Study Says," March 14, 1994.

David Boesel, "The Street Value of the GED Diploma," *Phi Delta Kappan*, September 1, 1998.

William Lowe Boyd, "What Makes Ghetto Schools Succeed or Fail?" *Teachers College Record*, Spring 1991.

David S. Broder, " 'Quality Managed' Schools Soar," *News-Journal*, Daytona Beach, FL, July 14, 1999.

Richard J. Coley, *Dreams Deferred: High School Dropouts in the United States*. Policy Information Report. Princeton, NJ: Educational Testing Service, 1995.

Hunter Downing, Otis LoVette, and Peter Emerson, "An Investigation of At-Risk Students' Reasons for Staying in School," *Journal of Humanistic Education and Development*, December 1994.

Dropout Prevention: Nowhere to Go. Distributed by AGC/United Learning, Evanston, IL, 1991. Videocassette.

Economist, "Virtual Jobs in Motown," March 26, 1994.

Kitty Kelly Epstein, "Case Studies in Dropping Out and Dropping Back In," *Journal of Education*, vol. 174, no. 3, 1992.

Robert W. Glover and Ray Marshall, "Improving the School-to-Work Transition of American Adolescents," *Teachers College Record*, Spring 1993.

Christine Gober-Huntington, "A Brighter Horizon," *Thrust for Educational Leadership*, November/December 1995.

Susan Headden, "The Hispanic Dropout Mystery," *U.S. News & World Report*, October 20, 1997.

Lori Horvitz, "Students Find Help, Hope," *Orlando Sentinel*, November 22, 1998.

———, "Tech Academy Is Hot Off Presses," *Orlando Sentinel*, March 6, 1999.

"I Dropped Out. But I Didn't Think It Would Be Like This." Distributed by Cambridge Research Group, Charleston, WV, 1989. Videocassette.

Job Corps, *Listen Up*, "Three Amigas," Winter 1999.

Job Corps, *Success Lasts a Lifetime* (brochure).

Job Corps, *Your Guide to the New Job Corps* (brochure).

Will J. Jordan, Julia Lara, and James M. McPartland, "Exploring the Causes of Early Dropout Among Race-Ethnic and Gender Groups," *Youth & Society*, September 1996.

Kathleen L. Kaminski, "Rural Dropouts: A Casual Comparison," *Education*, Summer 1993.

Yolanda G. Martinez and Ann Cranston-Gingras, "Migrant Farmworker Students and the Educational Process: Barriers to High School Completion," *High School Journal*, October 1, 1996.

The Merrow Report, PBS documentary, "Lost in Translation: Latinos, Schools and Society," October 4, 1998.

National Dropout Prevention Center, "Chances of Becoming a Professional NBA Basketball Player," fact sheet, Clemson University, Clemson, SC.

Beth Spenciner Rosenthal, DSW, ACSW, "The Influence of Social Support on School Completion Among Haitians," *Social Work in Education*, January 1995.

Jeanne Jacoby Smith, "Anatomy of a High School Dropout," *The World & I*, July 1998.

U.S. Department of Education, National Center for Education Statistics (NCES), *Dropout Rates in the United States, 1996*. NCES 98-250, by Marilyn M. McMillen and Phillip Kaufman, Washington, DC: GPO, 1997.

Internet Sources

Center for Effective Collaboration and Practice (CECP): Improving Services to Children and Youth with Emotional and Behavioral Problems, "Paying Now or Paying Later," April 14, 1999. www.air.org/cecp/resources/schfail/paying.html.

Marty Duckenfield, "The Performance of At-Risk Youth as Tutors," National Dropout Prevention Center. www. dropoutprevention.org/effstrat/performance.htm.

———, "Service Learning: Real Dropout Prevention," National Dropout Prevention Center. www.dropoutprevention.org/effstrat/goopre.htm.

ETS Research, "Dreams Deferred: High School Dropouts Face Bleak Future," June 2, 1995. www.ets.org/research/pic/pr/dropouts.html.

SFC Douglas Ide, "Challenging At-Risk Youth," *Soldiers*, November 1994. www.dtic.mil/soldiers/nov94/p42.html.

Learning & Serving: The Southern Service Learning Newsletter, "Kentucky Learn and Serve Goes to the State Fair!" Fall 1997. www.dropoutprevention.org/effstrat/S&LNews.htm.

Maj. Maria L. LoVasco, "Another Challenge," *On Guard*, April 1997. www.ngb.dtic.mil/grdnews/onguard/1997/apr/challeng.htm.

National Mentoring Partnership, "About Mentoring." www. mentoring.org/mentoring.html.

National Mentoring Partnership, "Find a Mentor." www. mentoring.org/youth.html.

The News-Times, "High School Dropouts Highest Among Minority Groups," June 23, 1997. www.newstimes.com/ archive97/jun2397/rgf.htm.

Penta County Vocational High School, "Career Opportunities, Secondary—High School." http://pentanet.k12.oh.us/home/ pc_hs.htm.

Wendy Schwartz, "New Information on Youth Who Drop Out: Why They Leave and What Happens to Them," KidSource OnLine, January 26, 1999. www.kidsource.com/ kidsource/content4/youth.drop.out.html.

——, "School Dropouts: New Information About an Old Problem," *ERIC Clearinghouse on Urban Education*. Digest Number 109, 1995. http://eric-web.tc.columbia.edu/digests/ dig109.html.

David Thomas, "Dropout Rates Remain Stable over Last Decade," National Center for Education Statistics (NCES) press release, December 17, 1997. http://nces.ed.gov/ Pressrelease/dropout.html.

U.S. Department of Education, Division of Vocational-Technical Education, "Career Guidance and Counseling and School-to-Work Opportunities." www.ed.gov/offices/OVAE/ cgcstw.html.

U.S. Department of Education, "Educational and Labor Market Performance of GED Recipients," Executive Summary, February 1998. http://inet.ed.gov/pubs/GED/execsum.html.

U.S. Department of Education, Office of Educational Research and Improvement (OERI), "Defining Dropouts: A Statistical Portrait," *Reaching the Goals: Goal 2—High School Completion*, March 1994. www.ed.gov/pubs/ ReachingGoals/Goal_2/Dropouts.html.

Index

Picture Credits

About the Author

Elizabeth Weiss Vollstadt is a freelance writer and a former teacher. She holds a B.A. from Adelphi University and an M.A. from John Carroll University, both in English. Her stories for young people have appeared in publications such as the *Highlights for Children* anthologies, *Children's Digest*, *Jack and Jill*, *My Friend*, and *The Christian Family Christmas Book*. She has taught English and writing to students from grade seven through college. She now lives in DeLand, Florida, with her husband, where she divides her time between writing and boating on the St. Johns River. This is her second book for Lucent's Teen Issues series.